Welcome . . .

Hello, I'm R.L. Stine. Welcome to part two of a very special *Nightmare Room* story.

It's about a girl named April Powers who joins eleven other kids on a tropical island. The kids are there to play survival games—for a prize of $100,000. But they soon discover that someone else is on the island, someone who doesn't *want* them to survive!

When I started to write this story, I realized that it was too big and too frightening to tell in one book. April's story had to be told in *three* books instead of one.

And so the THRILLOGY was born.

Welcome to my *special* nightmare . . .

PROLOGUE

April Powers watched as her teammates, Kristen, Anthony, and Marlin, ran to the end of the weathered wooden pier. Its gray pilings creaked and groaned with the pull of the tide.

"I can't believe this!" April shouted over the crashing waves. "They left us here!"

She had watched the boat pull away, the boat that had carried the twelve kids to this tropical island two weeks earlier.

"They took everything!" Marlin cried. "We're alone here! And there's no way home!"

"But they'll come back for us," Anthony said. "It's all a game, right? They wouldn't really leave us here all alone—would they?"

April shivered. Hugging herself, she turned and gazed down the beach to the eerie, blue rocks. The rocks glowed, even in the darkness.

We're not alone, she thought.

Something else lives here. Something evil.

She could feel it even now . . . watching her . . . waiting . . .

Waiting for the right moment to strike.

"We have to find a way out of here," April said. "We've got to get off this island—before it's too late."

Part One

A Tropical Island This Spring

Hugging herself tightly, April Powers stared out at the tossing ocean waves. A bolt of jagged lightning flashed on the horizon. In the sudden light, the water flared green, bright as day.

Thunder crackled in the distance. Lightning flickered, closer this time.

Shivering, April turned to her three friends. "That storm is heading this way," she muttered.

"Perfect," Kristen Wood said, shaking her head bitterly. "We're abandoned on this empty island. And now we're going to be washed away."

"Marks will come back for us," Anthony Thomas said. He pulled a beetle from his red hair and crushed it between his fingers. "He has to come back. This is probably some kind of test."

"I don't see any boats in the water," April replied, shivering again. She felt a heavy raindrop on her shoulder. Another one on the top of her head. "They took the boats and left us here. They're not coming back."

"It's a survival game," Anthony insisted. "Marks is the director of The Academy. He's a businessman, right? He's not going to abandon four kids on an island."

"But . . . what if something went terribly wrong?" April asked. "What if it was some kind of emergency? And he gathered up everyone he could—and split?"

Marlin Davis had been silent this whole time. He was hunched beside the others on the small dock, watching the waves grow higher, watching them crash onto the rocky shore.

He pulled off his baseball cap and scratched his head. "They did leave in an awful hurry," he said softly.

"But they took everything with them," Anthony said. "That means their escape was planned."

He brushed a raindrop off his forehead. "I'm telling you, guys, it's a game. Part of the Life Games. This is the bravery competition. So . . . don't panic."

"Don't panic?" April's words came out shriller than she had planned. "Don't panic? We have no food. No phones. No way to contact anybody."

Kristen placed a hand on April's trembling shoulder. "Are you sure there's no food?" she asked.

A deafening boom of thunder made all four of them jump. The rain came down harder, pattering noisily on the planks of the dock.

Marlin jumped to his feet. "Let's go check. Let's see what they left us."

Ducking their heads against the pouring rain, April and her friends ran off the dock, across the shore, and to the cabins and huts of The Academy Village. By the time they burst through the open mess hall door, they were soaked.

Marlin tried the light switch. He clicked it several times. "They must have turned off the generator," he said.

"Oh, great," April moaned. "No power at all."

Lightning flickered outside the window. April could see that the tables had been pushed against the wall. The chairs were all overturned.

"Did they leave anything in the kitchen?" Kristen asked. She was already halfway there, her wet sneakers sliding on the wooden floor.

April shook out her short brown hair as she trotted after her friend. This isn't happening, she thought.

It's the middle of the night. And I'm having a nightmare. I'm dreaming that Donald Marks took his assistants and the other kids and roared away on the only two boats.

Wake up, April, she urged herself. Please—wake up!

But no. She joined the others in the dark kitchen. Anthony had found a flashlight and was sending a darting circle of light around the room.

"Oh, wow. The shelves are bare," Kristen murmured.

"Try the fridge," Marlin said.

April pulled open the heavy metal door. Anthony beamed his light into the big refrigerator.

"Oh, gross!" April screamed. "I'm going to be sick!"

The beam of light from Anthony's flashlight trembled over the fat mouse, dead on its back on the bottom refrigerator shelf.

The creature's stomach had been clawed open—probably by a cat or a large bird. Red and yellow guts puddled around it. One tiny black eye dangled from its socket.

"At least we have dessert!" Marlin grinned.

"Shut the door," April moaned, hiding her eyes.

"Who would *do* that?" Kristen asked. "Someone had to pick up that dead mouse and drop it in the fridge."

"It's all a test," Anthony insisted. "Bravery, remember?"

"But what are we supposed to eat?" Kristen cried. "Are we supposed to pick berries? Are we supposed to catch fish with our hands?"

Her shoulders heaved up and down. She was shivering so hard, her voice quivered.

"Let's stay calm," Marlin said softly. "We're the best team—right? We're the survivors. We'll figure this out."

Marlin had been the team leader ever since the kids had arrived on the island. An African American, tall and athletic, with a great smile and a funny sense of humor, Marlin had been the one to keep the team together.

April felt really close to Marlin. When the others were putting her down, he stuck with her. She knew her teammates were still suspicious of her. A strange incident in the mess hall one morning had convinced them that April had evil powers.

Of all the crazy things, she thought.

The others had wanted to shut her out entirely. But Marlin stayed her friend. And now the four of them were alone on this island.

We have no choice now, April told herself. We *really* have to stick together.

"I think we'll all be able to think more clearly in the morning," Marlin said. "Let's head back to our cabins and—"

"And sleep?" Kristen cried shrilly. "How can we sleep when we know we're all alone here?"

"Marlin is right," April said. "We're soaked and we're exhausted. At least, if we go to our beds, we can get dry and warm up."

Jagged lightning crackled outside the window. The empty room exploded in light.

"Whoa. That was close!" April exclaimed.

"Maybe the storm will be over by morning," Marlin said, shaking his head. "Then we can make a plan."

"Yeah. A plan," Anthony repeated.

He had been insisting this was all a game. And now he was trying to sound brave. But April could hear the fear in his voice.

I'm frightened too, she thought. *I don't think this is a game. I think something is very wrong here.*

April was sure she would lie awake all night. But she fell asleep nearly as soon as her head hit the pillow.

She dreamed about home. Mom and Dad were at the dinner table with April's friend Pam. Pam sat in April's chair.

They were laughing and laughing. April was nowhere to be seen. "Pam, you're the best!" April's mom kept saying. "You're the best! Better than April. Better than April in every way!"

April awoke, feeling disturbed. The unhappy dream lingered in her mind.

Glancing across the cabin, she saw that Kristen had already left. She dragged herself up, washed her face in the sink against the wall, pulled on khaki shorts, a green midriff T, and her sneakers. And hurried to the mess hall.

The rain had stopped, but gray clouds still covered the sky. The morning air felt cool and damp. The cabins, the grass, the dirt path to the beach—everything shimmered wetly.

The storm had really messed up the ocean, April noticed. She watched wave after foamy wave pound the shore. Her stomach grumbled hungrily as she made her way to the mess hall.

"'Morning," she muttered as she stepped inside. Her three friends had pulled a table into the center of the room and sat around it.

Kristen looked nearly as bedraggled as the night before. She hadn't bothered to brush her blond-brown hair, which fell in limp tangles around her face.

Anthony and Marlin were excitingly discussing something. "The boat has to be there," Marlin said. "I know they didn't take it."

"No way. I'll bet it's gone," Anthony said.

"What boat?" April asked, joining them.

"Remember the little red motorboat?" Marlin replied. "The one Marks's assistants used to go around the island?"

"Yes!" April cried. "Of course. It's tied up by the rocks, right?"

"It's not that far from here to the main island," Marlin said. "That little boat is pretty speedy. It can take us there easily. And I think there is a radio on it."

"If we need to, we can radio for help!" Kristen said, smiling for the first time.

"Very cool. What are we waiting for?" April asked.

They found the boat on its side on the outcropping of blue rocks. Marlin grabbed it and tilted it upright.

"Is it wrecked?" Anthony asked. He grabbed the side of the boat and rocked it. "Seems okay."

"No damage as far as I can tell," Marlin said.

"Excellent!" Kristen cried, pumping her fist in the air.

Marlin opened the cap on the outboard motor and gazed inside. "Guess what? A full tank of gas!"

April and the others cheered. "Maybe our luck is changing," she said.

She grabbed the microphone and turned the dial on the radio. "Hello? Hello?" She let out a disappointed cry. "It's silent."

"Maybe the batteries got wet," Marlin said. "We don't need it. Let's get in the water."

"Yeah. Before it starts to pour," Kristen said, frowning up at the clouds.

The four of them dragged the boat down to the shore. The outboard motor bounced heavily behind it.

Tall waves swept over the rocks as they pulled the boat into the water. They could feel the strong current pulling away from the shore.

"The ocean is so rough," Anthony said, biting his bottom lip. "Think this little boat can make it?"

"It should be calmer once we get past the breaking waves," Marlin replied. "But if anyone wants to stay back . . ."

"No way!" April cried.

They scrambled into the boat. It was a tight squeeze, but they just fit.

The boat rocked wildly on the tossing waves.

April felt her stomach lurch. "Whoa—!" she cried out as the boat tipped almost straight up.

Then it dropped down with a hard *slap* on the water.

At the back of the bobbing boat, Marlin turned to the motor. "Here comes the big test!" he shouted over the roar of the waves. "Will it start?"

April crossed her fingers on both hands. Please work, she prayed. Please!

The boat rocked hard again and spun against the onrushing waves. Marlin pressed the ignition button.

The engine coughed. A low rumble. And then it kicked in, roaring over the rush of the waves.

"Yes!" Marlin shouted, pumping his fist in the air. "We have liftoff!"

April and the others cheered. They held on tight as Marlin turned the boat away from the shore.

Wave after wave battered them.

It's like they're trying to push us back, April thought.

The motor coughed, then roared again. The boat bounced high over the waves.

"Yes! Yes! We're OUTTA here!" April cheered.

"Hold on!" Marlin yelled, his hand bouncing on the control. "Hold on tight!"

The boat struggled to leap over the roaring waves.

April shut her eyes and gripped the sides of the boat as a powerful force spun the boat around.

Suddenly, they began to spin crazily . . . faster . . . faster. . . . Whirling helplessly. . . . Picking up speed as if caught in a spinning whirlpool.

"Why is it doing this?" April cried.

"I—I can't control it!" Marlin screamed.

Dizziness swept over April. This is *crazy*! she thought. The waves aren't spinning us around. The waves are rolling straight to shore.

What kind of a current are we caught in? Why is the boat spinning like this?

And then she saw the tall blue rocks loom above them.

"NOOOOO!" Another scream tore from her throat as the boat spun hard—and crashed against the rocks. April heard a shattering *craaaack* as the boat splintered apart.

She threw her hands up, as if reaching for something to hold on to. But her hands grabbed only air. And she flew from the boat, screaming. Screaming . . .

And in that instant, the world turned upside down. The sky stretched beneath her feet now.

Tossed by the force of the crash, April plunged beneath the water. The shock paralyzed her. She let the force of her fall carry her down.

The cold, wet world stretched green all around her. So green, she thought.

Where is the boat? Where are my friends?

Can I move?

And then she snapped back to her senses. And realized she *had* to move.

She raised her arms and kicked—and forced herself to the surface. She bobbed up, gasping for air. The waves tossed her hard.

"Help me!" She heard a cry. Recognized Anthony's voice.

But he seemed so far away.

"Help me!"

Paddling hard, April turned toward the voice. But a wave roared over her.

Choking, sputtering, she was thrown beneath the surface, back into the green world.

No! She forced herself up. The current pulled her away from shore—then pushed her hard to the rocks.

How can I swim in this? she wondered. *The waves are so powerful—and the undertow . . .*

"Help!" She heard Anthony's cry again, closer this time.

April turned in time to see the shattered boat roll forward, carried on a high wave.

It's coming right at me! she realized. *It's going to hit me!*

She sucked in a deep breath—and dove under the surface again. She saw the dark shadow of the boat roll over her.

When she pulled herself up, the boat bobbed beside her, broken and bent.

April saw Kristen climbing onto the rocks onshore with the radio from the boat in her hands.

Then she spotted Anthony, fighting the waves, struggling to stay afloat. He uttered another cry for help, weaker this time. And then she let out a terrified gasp as he disappeared under a rushing whitecap.

With a groan, April threw herself toward Anthony. "I . . . I'm coming!" she choked out. A wave crashed over her, filling her mouth with salty foam.

Choking, she pulled herself through the tossing waters.

Yes! Anthony bobbed up from below the surface, thrashing, sputtering.

Using all her strength, April forced herself forward. And now she had her arm around Anthony's chest and was swimming hard, struggling to pull Anthony to shore.

"Come on, Anthony! We can make it! We can make it!" April groaned.

Her arms ached. She struggled to breathe. Holding on to Anthony, she fought the waves.

The rocks rose up in front of her. And then, Kristen was grabbing April by the shoulders and pulling them both onto the rocks. "You okay?" Kristen asked in a tiny voice. "Are you?"

April brushed the salty water from her eyes and swept her hands back through her dark hair. She opened her mouth to answer Kristen. But she was panting too hard to speak.

Anthony sprawled lifelessly on his back. His eyes were shut. His head tilted at a strange, awkward angle.

"Anthony?" April cried. "Anthony? Can you open your eyes? Can you hear me?"

He opened his mouth in a low groan. Slowly, he pulled himself up to a sitting position. Water ran down his face.

"Anthony?" April cried. "Say something! Tell us you're okay!"

He opened his mouth. And then his eyes bulged wide. "Something is . . . wrong," he choked out.

Then he started to cough. Cough after wracking cough shook his body. His eyes bulged even wider.

Something pink bubbled in his mouth.

He coughed harder, a choking cough.

And a slimy pink blob flew onto his lap.

"A jellyfish!" April cried.

"Ohhhh, gross!" Kristen groaned.

Anthony coughed again. His whole body heaved. Another fat pink jellyfish slid from his open mouth. It plopped softly on top of the first jellyfish.

April and Kristen gaped in horror as Anthony's slender body twisted and heaved. Another jellyfish bubbled in his mouth, then dropped to the rocky ground.

Finally, Anthony's body relaxed. He breathed heavily, wheezing with each breath. He stared down wide-eyed at the pile of jellyfish he had coughed up and moaned.

Staring at the glistening fat jellyfish, a wave of nausea swept over April. She shut her eyes and held her breath.

"Marlin—" April suddenly remembered. "Where is he?"

Kristen pulled April to her feet. She pointed around the curve in the rock wall. "He must have swum to shore over there."

"We . . . have to find him." As she tried to run, April felt waterlogged, heavy. Her legs didn't want to move.

She turned and saw the boat spinning in the water again. Spinning crazily, as if moved by an invisible force.

And then suddenly, it tilted straight up—and slid down. The boat sank beneath the surface and didn't return.

April's soaked sneakers thudded over the rocks as she followed Kristen around the curve.

April glanced around the shore. "I don't see him," she muttered. "Hey—Marlin?" April called. "Marlin?"

"He has to be here. Where did he go?" Kristen asked in a trembling voice.

Anthony staggered toward them. "Do you see him?"

April shook her head.

"I know I saw him swimming to shore," Anthony said.

"Then where is he?" Kristen demanded shrilly. "He's the best swimmer of all of us! The best!"

April's throat tightened with fear. She glanced over the rocks, glowing dully under the cloudy sky.

No sign of him.

She turned back to the water. Wave after wave rolled to the shore, sending up white sprays of foam.

No sign of him in the ocean either.

A chill of fear ran down April's back.

He's gone, she thought. He has disappeared.

April kept staring out at the ocean. Was that Marlin's head bobbing behind that rolling wave?

No. Just a seagull, out for a wild ride.

"Where is he?" she murmured. "Where?"

Shivering, Kristen hugged herself. "Maybe we should go back to the village and change into dry clothes," she suggested. "Then we can search for him."

"No!" Anthony cried. He was on his feet now, his pale face almost ghostlike. His wet clothes clung to him. His shoes sloshed as he made his way over the sand to them.

"We have to find him—now," Anthony insisted. "I'm not going back until we find him."

"You're right," April agreed. And then her voice broke. "I—I just don't understand it. You saw him swimming to shore?"

Anthony nodded.

"So where could he be?" April asked.

Kristen and Anthony stared back at her blankly.

"Maybe he saw something somewhere?" Kristen suggested weakly.

"He definitely wouldn't go back into the water," April said. "There was no reason to go back in."

"That means he's definitely onshore," Kristen said. "Maybe we should go back to camp and wait for him. April, you know how he wanders off sometimes. You had to go rescue him on the rocks, remember? That's how we won the loyalty contest?"

"I . . . have a bad feeling about this," April said softly. She pulled a chunk of seaweed from the collar of her T-shirt and tossed it to the ground.

"What kind of bad feeling?" Kristen asked, shivering, water dripping off her.

"We don't have time for bad feelings," Anthony said, shaking his head. "We've got to find Marlin." He spun around and began following the beach as it curved in front of the rocks.

April and Kristen trooped after him.

"Marlin? Hey, Marlin? Maaaaaarlinnnnnn?" They shouted his name as they walked.

April felt a cold raindrop on her forehead. "He couldn't have gone far," she said.

After a few minutes, Kristen stopped. "Maybe we should split up. You know, search in different directions."

"Maybe one of us should search the rocks. And one of us should search the beach. And one of us—"

"No," Anthony interrupted. "I think we should stick together—just for safety."

Kristen turned to April. "I agree with Anthony," April said.

The rain started to patter down, pushed by a gusting wind. They climbed the sloping hill of blue rocks and gazed down from the top.

No sign of Marlin.

Then, trudging wearily over the wet sand, heads bowed in the rain, they searched the beach again.

No Marlin.

April sighed. "If he *is* waiting for us back at the village, I'll *kill* him!" she exclaimed.

She picked up the radio Kristen had rescued and started to carry it to the village. She thought about how nice it would be to change into dry clothes and get under some shelter. But her thoughts kept returning to Marlin.

"I don't know why I bothered saving that," Kristen said, walking beside April. "It's not going to work. We don't have any batteries."

April let out a sigh. She pulled back her arm and prepared to heave it into the ocean.

"No—wait." Anthony grabbed her arm. "I have some batteries in my cabin. The ones I used for my tape player."

April tucked the radio back under her arm. "I'm so exhausted, I can't think straight."

The dock came into view, still empty, still bobbing in the rough waves. They turned and started to jog to the cabins.

"Marlin? Are you here?" April shouted. "Marlin?"

No reply.

Trudging through the rain, they searched every building. The cabins were dark and empty.

Anthony's pale features tightened with fear. "How could he disappear into thin air?" he asked in a tiny, frightened voice.

They sloshed through the puddled sand to their cabins. April squeezed her hair. It drizzled water like a soaked sponge.

She dried it as best she could and changed into a pair of snug leggings and a heavy sweatshirt. She realized she was shivering.

"Why is it suddenly so cold?" she asked Kristen.

Kristen shrugged. She had pulled on two T-shirts and a vest over faded jeans. "At least the rain has finally stopped," she said.

They made their way to the mess hall. It was early afternoon, but the cloud-filled sky was dark as night.

"Oh!"

April saw a boy walking quickly toward the back of the mess hall. At first, she thought it was Marlin, and her heart jumped.

But then he turned around, and April saw that it was Anthony wearing one of Marlin's jackets.

Marlin, where are you? April wondered, gazing

toward the ocean. There are only three of us left, and it's very scary without you.

Anthony huddled over the electrical generator. "This can't be too complicated," he said. "Let's try this."

He flipped a switch on the side. Silence. And then the generator hummed to life.

April heard a whirring sound inside the big metal structure.

And then the whole thing rattled and hummed as it came to life.

"Yes! I'm a genius!" Anthony exclaimed. He slapped the two girls high-fives.

Kristen rolled her eyes. "Anthony, all you did was flick a switch."

"But now we have power," he said excitedly. "We have electricity."

He turned and ran to the front of the mess hall. April and Kristen hurried after him.

Inside, he clicked the switch, and the ceiling light flashed on. "Yes!"

He turned to them, his eyes wide. "Where is the boat radio? Here. I brought batteries."

April groaned. "I left it in the cabin."

She took off, running to her cabin. It was suddenly very still out. No breeze at all. Not a leaf quivered on the palm trees at the edge of the forest.

Halfway to the cabin, she stopped.

Her skin prickled. Why did she have the feeling someone was watching her?

"Marlin?"

She gazed into the trees. No. No one there.

Shaking off the strange feeling, she ran to the cabin, picked up the radio, and carried it to Kristen and Anthony.

Anthony slid the batteries into the back. The three of them huddled around as he turned the power switch. The radio crackled to life.

"We're outta here!" Anthony declared. "We'll contact someone on the main island. We'll explain what's happening. And they'll be here in minutes."

He grinned at the two girls. "What's the first thing you're going to eat when we get to some food?"

"Pizza!" Both April and Kristen answered at once. They burst out laughing.

Then all three of them turned back to the radio. Anthony handed April the microphone. Slowly, he began turning the dial, searching for a frequency.

"What should I say?" April asked. "Should I say *mayday* or something, like in the movies?"

"Just say hello," Kristen answered.

"Yeah. Keep saying hello until someone answers," Anthony said.

April stared at the crackling radio. The microphone trembled in her hand.

She raised the mike to her mouth. "Hello? Hello? Hello? Can anyone hear me?"

The radio whistled. The sound rose and fell as Anthony turned the dial.

"Hello? Hello?" April realized she was shouting into the microphone. "Hello? Anyone? Please?"

All three of them snapped to attention when they heard a voice.

A woman's voice. Very distant. Almost buried in the crackling static.

"Hello?" April called to the woman. "Hello? Can you hear me?"

April struggled to hear. But the woman's voice disappeared behind the static.

"Hello? Can you hear me?" April turned to Anthony. "Can you turn the volume up?"

Anthony shook his head. "I've got it cranked up as high as it will go."

And then the static faded. April and the others could hear the woman clearly. Her voice lifted and fell.

"She's singing!" Kristen exclaimed.

Yes.

The woman was singing in a low, throaty voice.

Singing a slow, sad song in a foreign language April didn't recognize.

"What's going on?" April cried, staring at the radio speaker. And then she froze.

She recognized the voice.

She had heard that voice—here on the island.

A chill spread over the back of her neck. "It . . . it's the same woman," April murmured.

Anthony's mouth dropped open.

Kristen turned to her. "Excuse me?"

"It's the singing I heard before," April said. "The same song, the same strange words."

They listened to the song, so slow and sad. No music. Just a woman singing alone.

Kristen shuddered. "Change the frequency—quick," she told Anthony.

April didn't wait for him. She grabbed the dial and turned it.

They heard static again.

And then the woman returned, singing in her low, throaty voice.

April gave the dial a hard turn. "Hello? Hello?" she called into the microphone.

The whistling and static faded. And the woman was back again.

"No!" April cried.

She turned the dial.

The woman was still there, singing her strange, sad song.

"Please!" April cried, feeling herself lose control. "Please—get off! Stop! Stop singing!"

Another frequency. The woman was there too.

Another.

The woman continued her song.

"Stop it! Stop it!" April screamed.

"She's everywhere!" Kristen cried. "She's on every frequency!"

Anthony shook his head, his face twisted in confusion. "But—that's impossible!" he muttered.

And then through the tiny radio speaker, they heard the woman start to laugh. A deep, cold, cruel laugh.

"Turn it off!" Kristen cried, holding her ears. "April—turn it off!"

April clicked off the radio and tossed the microphone to the floor.

But to their horror, the laughter continued.

Icy laughter, sharp as icicles . . . echoing off the walls, ringing in their ears.

April pulled the blanket up to her chin. Why is it so cold? she wondered.

This is a tropical island. It's supposed to be summer all year long.

She shut her eyes and tried not to think about anything at all.

The rest of the day had gone by in a blur.

When the woman's terrifying laughter finally stopped, April and her friends tried the radio again. They knew it was their only hope.

But now it fell completely silent. Not even whistles or static.

Chilled, they had tried to light a fire in the mess hall fireplace. But every time the logs started to catch, a powerful wind blew down the chimney and put the fire out.

April, Kristen, and Anthony stared at the fireplace in disbelief.

"It's like . . . we're *cursed* or something," Anthony muttered, his voice cracking.

"Still think this is part of the Life Games competition?" Kristen asked him.

Anthony only shrugged in reply.

They hadn't eaten all day. In the mess hall kitchen, they made a desperate search of every cabinet.

They actually cheered when April found a small box of crackers on a bottom shelf. They divided the crackers evenly, then devoured them in seconds.

"What about tomorrow?" April had asked, licking the last salty crumb off her finger.

"We'll think of something," Kristen said softly. "I know we will."

Anthony stared into the dark fireplace and didn't say a word.

Now, late at night, April shivered in her cot, her stomach growling and churning. We should win the bravery contest just for surviving today, she thought bitterly.

And then her thoughts turned even darker: Will anyone come to rescue us? How long can we survive without any food?

She wondered what her parents were doing right now. And she thought about her friend Pam. Pam had been so jealous, so eager to go to the island.

Pam doesn't know how lucky she is, April thought.

And then the singing began again.

April raised her head from the pillow and listened.

Yes. The same song. The same slow, sad song.

The woman's voice was soft and distant, but April could hear it so clearly.

Where is it coming from? April wondered. Is the woman on this island?

The sound sent shivers down her back. The window was closed tight, but the sad melody floated into the cabin, louder now, as if the woman were standing right outside.

"Hey, Kristen?" April whispered. "Kristen—are you awake? Do you hear it?"

Across the cabin, Kristen stirred and rolled over. April could hear her breathing, steady and slow.

"Kristen?"

She's sound asleep, April realized.

The singing floated through the cabin. It swirled around April. It seemed to blanket her.

She shoved her hands out, as if trying to push the song away.

But the woman's voice wrapped itself around her. It seemed to pull April. She could feel herself being tugged from the bed.

"No. No," she protested in a whisper. She tugged the blanket high and covered her ears with both hands.

But she couldn't shut it out.

The woman's voice is calling to me, April realized. She is trying to pull me to her. To pull me from my bed.

No. I won't go. I won't . . .

April felt a tingling on her back. The tingle quickly became an itch. It spread down her arms, her legs.

What is happening? she gasped.

Her whole body itched.

She heaved away the blanket and jumped out of bed.

"Ohhhhhh, sick." A groan escaped her throat.

She stared down in horror at her bed. Crawling with bugs. Fat brown beetles swarmed over her pillow, over her sheet.

April slapped her arms. Scratched her legs. She had slept in her clothes, but the beetles had burrowed under them, nesting in her skin.

Slapping and scraping them away, she did a wild dance across the floor. Frantically, she pulled them off the back of her neck. Batted them from her hair. Clawed them from her scalp.

And all the while, the woman's song continued, drawing her away, tugging her, inviting her. . . .

And now April was sliding on her sneakers.

And making her way past Kristen's cot.

And pushing open the cabin door, closing it so quietly behind her.

No. I don't want to do this. I don't want to go out.

But she couldn't help herself. April stepped into the cold, still night. So still, nothing moving. Not a palm leaf or a blade of grass.

As still as a nightmare, April thought.

That's it. I'm walking through a nightmare.

The fat, swarming beetles . . . the woman's strange singing . . . all a nightmare.

But she couldn't stop herself.

"No. I won't do this!" she whispered. She wrapped her arms around the slender trunk of a palm tree. I won't let go. You can't pull me away.

The woman's voice rang louder in her ears. The song repeated, pulling her . . . pulling her.

Her arms slipped away from the tree. She barely saw the cabins pass by as her feet carried her to the beach. The little dock stood empty, and so still. Even the ocean didn't appear to move.

No waves. No sound of water rushing over the shore.

As if everything had frozen in time. As if the whole world had come to a stop.

Except for the beating of April's heart. And the scrape of her shoes on sand as she made her way along the silent, empty beach.

No. I want to go back. I have to go back to the cabin.

The woman sang so sadly. Her voice was hoarse and soft, as if she were very, very old.

April crossed the sand and stepped onto the blue rocks. The rocks shimmered even though there was no moon in the sky.

And as she started to climb, a shudder of terror shook her body.

The fear inside her—the fear she had been holding in since she left the cabin—broke free.

April wanted to open her mouth wide and scream and scream. She wanted to turn and run. Run as fast as she could, away from these eerie blue rocks. Away from this terrifying place.

But she couldn't scream.

And she couldn't run.

She could only climb the slippery rock hill, as if floating. As if being pulled by a powerful force.

And then . . . then . . . as the rock caves came into view . . . a strong aroma made her stop. A stench of rotting fish, of mildew and dirt and decay . . . the stench of death.

The smell overwhelmed April. It washed over her, so thick and putrid, she thought she could *feel* it on her skin.

She started to gag. She tried holding her breath. But the powerful stench was *inside* her now.

Gagging, she staggered forward. And suddenly, the force seemed to let go of her. To drop her.

The singing stopped.

And April collapsed to the hard surface. Her legs folded.

The shimmering glow of the rocks faded. And she fell in a faint, a dead faint, sprawled over the rocks.

As silent and still as the rest of the world.

April opened her eyes and gazed up at the woman.

How long had she been unconscious? How long had she been on her back on these cold, damp rocks?

How did I get here? April wondered, feeling dazed and weak.

It took a lot of effort to raise her head off the hard stone. She blinked, trying to clear her mind. Trying to remember . . .

The woman smiled down at her, a cold, unfriendly smile. April saw herself reflected in the woman's strange, silvery eyes.

The hood of the woman's dark blue cloak had fallen back. And her long blond-brown hair had fallen free.

She was attractive, April thought, with a broad forehead, full red lips, and those cat-shaped, silvery eyes.

"Who . . . are you?" April whispered.

The woman didn't reply. Instead, her smile grew

wider and she lowered her head over April. Brought her head down closer . . . closer . . . and pressed her mouth against April's.

Lightning flashed in the sky. The woman's face flickered in the eerie light.

What is she *doing* to me? April wondered, panic freezing her in place. Why is she doing this?

April felt the woman's cold lips against her face. So cold, they stung her mouth.

As the woman pressed harder, April's body lost all its warmth. Her muscles stiffened from an icy chill that ran through her.

Choking, she gasped to breathe.

She tried to turn away, struggled to squirm free.

She . . . she's sucking my breath! April realized.

Bright white lightning flickered again.

The woman's eyes grew wide and her blond eyebrows rose up on her forehead as she raised her head. Then lowered it again. And pressed her mouth to April's.

Sucking . . . sucking her breath away.

This is sick . . . sick! April thought. And a spasm of horror shook her body.

The face loomed above her. The woman didn't make a sound.

Her lips remained cold and hard against April's.

No—please . . . April silently begged. Please, leave me just a little breath. Just a little life.

April tried to shove the woman away. She tried to kick. She tried to roll.

But she could feel a crushing force holding her in place.

The woman lowered her face once again. The silvery cat eyes glowed brightly. Lightning flashed.

And the woman whispered in April's ear. . . .

"What scares you the most? Tell me, daughter—what scares you the most?"

"I have waited a long time for this moment. I knew you would be drawn back to me," the woman whispered. "Now I will have my revenge."

The woman pulled the blue hood over her blond-brown hair. She seemed to disappear into the cloak, to slip into its darkness.

Beneath the hood, the woman's silvery eyes glowed as she lowered her face over April one more time.

"Please," April begged. "Please don't take my breath." Once again she pushed her arms up, trying to shove the woman away.

She saw the woman's pale white hand rise over her. Long, bony fingers, gnarled and bent.

The fingers pressed against April's forehead. At first they felt cold. But then April felt a sizzling heat.

And then the strange pale face faded. And the sky appeared to fall over April, covering her in darkness.

Flat on her back, she felt herself growing light-headed.

I'm fading away, she realized. I can't think . . . can't feel.

A loud shout cleared April's mind.

Fighting off waves of dizziness, April turned her head—and saw . . . Kristen.

Kristen! Eyes wild. Hair blowing around her face. Dark eyes wide with excitement.

With a scream of fury, Kristen threw herself onto the cloaked woman. She wrapped her arms around the woman's waist—and shoved her away from April.

The woman's mouth dropped open in a grunt of surprise. Her hood slid off as she fell back.

The two wrestled furiously, groaning and crying out.

They rolled to the hard stone ground and continued their battle.

April pushed herself to a sitting position. Her body felt as heavy as stone. Her head still spun with dizziness.

The woman chanted some strange-sounding words. Kristen flew backward. Her body slammed against a rock wall. She cried out—kicking her arms and legs. But her body seemed bound to the rocks—held there by some invisible force.

"No!" April cried. She forced herself up . . . up . . . and threw herself onto the woman. Joined the fight. She grabbed the woman's arms and tried to tug them off Kristen.

All three of them wrestled on the rocks, screaming, groaning, struggling.

And then . . . there were only two of them.

Kristen and April sprawled beside each other on the ground. The blue-cloaked woman was gone.

Shaking her head, Kristen pulled herself up, panting hard. "Almost . . ." she choked. "I almost had her."

"Where is she?" April whispered, struggling to find her voice. "Where did she go?"

Kristen didn't have time to answer.

"Congratulations, you two!" The girls heard a man shout. "You won!"

"The contest is over!" Donald Marks called. "You're the winners!"

Both girls jumped to their feet as Donald Marks appeared. Running hard, his bald head gleaming in the blue light off the rocks. The huge man tromped heavily as he ran, his fists pumping the air.

"Kristen, where did that woman go?" April repeated.

Kristen stared straight ahead and didn't answer.

"I said you won! Aren't you excited?" Marks ran up to them. He stared at them, sweat pouring down his forehead. "What are you two doing out here?"

Her heart pounding, April stared hard at him. She struggled to think.

She suddenly found herself wrapped in a damp fog. The fog swirled around her.

She could feel it wash over her—wash *through* her.

A cold, cleansing fog.

It disappeared as fast as it had come.

April and Kristen gazed blankly at each other. Almost as if seeing each other for the first time.

"I don't remember," she finally answered Marks. "I don't remember why we came out here."

Kristen frowned and shook her head. "I don't remember either," she said shakily. "It's the strangest thing."

A grin spread over Marks's round face. "At least you're okay!" he boomed. "And we have a winner! Your team has won the bravery contest!"

April and Kristen exchanged glances.

"You mean . . . this was all part of the competition?" April asked.

Marks nodded, still grinning. "We've been watching you the whole time. And you two girls showed true bravery by venturing out here in the middle of the night. Congratulations, your team has won a hundred thousand dollars!"

"Whoa!" April cried. "You're not kidding? A hundred thousand dollars? I—I don't believe it!"

A smile slowly spread over Kristen's face. She slapped April a high-five, then hugged her.

April stared hard at Marks. She still felt as if she were gazing through a thick fog. Her whole body was trembling with the effort to stand up.

Why did she feel so weak?

What were she and Kristen doing out in the middle of the night in front of the rock caves?

She couldn't remember.

Marks placed an arm on her shoulder. "April? Are you okay? You don't seem very excited to have won so much money!"

"I . . . I am," she said. "I guess I'm shocked. When you left the island, I thought you weren't coming back. I really thought that . . ." Her voice trailed off.

And then she remembered something else. "Marlin," she said. "Mr. Marks—Marlin is missing. This afternoon, he—"

"We found him," Marks interrupted. He turned and pointed down the rock hill. "On the other side of the island. Marlin is okay. A few broken ribs."

Kristen gasped. "But—what was he doing all the way over there?"

Marks shrugged his broad shoulders. "Rick and Abby are taking care of him. They've called for a chopper to take him to the main island."

"But—what happened to him?" April demanded.

"We'd better hurry," Marks said. "Anthony is waiting at the dock. Let's get to the boat and find you some food to eat. You must be starving."

April nodded. *I haven't eaten in two days,* she realized. *I guess that's why I feel so weak.*

Marks glanced at the dark cave opening behind them for a second. Then he turned and motioned for them to follow as he led the way back to the village.

April and Kristen hurried to their cabin to pack their bags. "I can't believe we're getting out of here!" April exclaimed.

Kristen glanced up from her suitcase. "Hey—what's that on your head?" she asked.

April turned to her. "Huh?" She moved to the mirror on the wall. "Where?"

Kristen stepped up beside her. "On your temple," she said. She pulled April's hair back.

And they both stared at the mark on April's temple.

"Did you always have a birthmark there?" Kristen asked, studying it.

"No," April answered, gazing into the mirror. "It—it's blue," she stammered.

"It looks just like a moon," Kristen said. "A blue crescent moon."

April pressed her fingers against it. It felt hot to the touch. Burning hot.

How did I get that? she wondered.

What does it mean?

Part Two

The Year 1680

Ravenswoode, a Tiny English Village

Deborah Andersen lay on her bed, staring at a black spider as it slowly zigzagged down the wall beside her bedroom window. She touched the cold whitewashed stone wall, trailing her finger along the spider's path.

She concentrated all her thoughts on the tiny black creature. A spider in the house was said to be good luck.

Good luck.

With a sigh, Deborah pressed her thumb against the spider's hairy body—and crushed it against the wall. Dark brown blood seeped from its flattened belly.

Good luck cannot help me now, Deborah thought bitterly. My life is over.

The villagers had accused her of witchcraft. And now she faced a punishment worse than death.

She huddled in her room in the small cottage she shared with her mother. Deborah knew these could be her last moments in this cottage, the house where she was born. But she could not find comfort in them. She hated the ugly village and its pinched, mean people, but she was terrified of what lay ahead of her too—terrified of the unknown.

Alderman Harrison's words rang in her ears. . . .

"Deborah Andersen, in our great mercy we have spared you death," Harrison had pronounced. "But you must leave this village immediately—never to return. You will be taken to Plymouth. There you will board a cargo ship. The ship will carry you across the sea to an island in the new world—a tropical island where no people live."

"But, sir—" Deborah had begun to protest.

"You are sentenced to live the rest of your life alone," Harrison declared. "Alone on an island that no one will ever visit. Alone, where you cannot harm any of our good people with your witchcraft."

"But I am not a witch!" Deborah had cried. "I have no powers. I am not a witch!"

But no one—no one in the entire village—believed her.

The day before, an evil spell had been cast on the Alderman's son, Aaron Harrison. To everyone's horror, the boy had been turned into a chicken—a chicken with Aaron's wavy blond hair growing out of the top of its head.

An angry mob dragged Deborah from her cottage and accused her of the crime. That night the village burned mysteriously, with flames as cold as ice.

This is Deborah's evil work again, the villagers shouted. The witch's revenge!

And why did they accuse her? Why did they blame her for all the troubles in the village? What made them so certain that Deborah was a witch?

Since the day she was born, the village of Ravenswoode had been cursed with unexplained illness, terrible storms, and ruined crops—one strange, unfortunate event after another. The once-rich farming land had, in the twelve years of Deborah's life, turned to dust.

But to the villagers, the strongest proof of Deborah's witchcraft was the mark on her forehead. The blue crescent moon that floated over her right temple.

Deborah hugged herself tightly, trying to stop the violent tremors of fear that shook her body.

I don't want to leave my mother, she thought as hot tears rolled down her cheeks.

I don't want to spend my whole life all alone. I am not a witch. I am innocent!

I am a twelve-year-old girl with bad luck. Very bad luck, to be born in this wretched village.

And then, as she gazed out the window, she saw them.

She saw the orange flames of the torches dancing against the night sky. And then she saw the black outlines of the men carrying the torches.

They are coming for me, she realized.

They are coming to take me away.

Deborah jumped to her feet. Her head spun with fear.

"Mother!" she called.

Where was her mother? After dinner, Katherine had disappeared into the little room at the back of the house. Was she still back there?

"Mother—they are coming!" Deborah cried, her voice choked with panic. "Help me! Mother!"

She could hear the men's voices now. She could hear their boots thrashing heavily through the tall grass.

"Mother!"

Deborah stumbled from her room and ran to the back of the cottage. The fire had burned low in the hearth. A few purple embers glowed at the bottom.

"Mother! Help me!"

Deborah shoved open the door of the little room. She burst breathlessly inside. "Please—"

It took a few seconds for her eyes to adjust to the candlelight.

Then she saw her mother—and let out a scream of horror.

Deborah found her mother, Katherine, huddled on all fours in the dark room. Katherine knelt inside a circle painted on the dirt floor.

Black candles flickered around her, forming a six-pointed star.

Katherine was spreading blue dye over the corpse of a headless chicken. The chicken's head had been set on fire. It burned inside a smoke-filled jar.

Katherine gazed up at her daughter slowly, with a cold, faraway look Deborah had never seen before.

"N-no!" Deborah cried, trembling in the doorway. "YOU are the witch! YOU! How can this be? Mother—YOU have cast all the spells of evil!"

Katherine continued to stare coldly at her daughter, but she didn't reply. She gripped the jar of blue dye tightly in her hands.

"*Why,* Mother?" Deborah screamed, hands pressed to her cheeks. "Why did you let them blame me? Why did you let them blame your own daughter—when it was YOU all along?"

A loud crash from the front of the house made Deborah scream.

Katherine jumped to her feet.

"They are here!" Deborah wailed. "They are here to take me away. Help me, Mother. Tell them the truth—please!"

She could hear the heavy tromping of the men's boots on the floor, coming closer.

"I am sorry, daughter," Katherine whispered. "But I have no choice."

And then she raised the jar—and splashed blue dye down the front of Deborah's dress.

Deborah uttered a startled cry. Katherine tossed the dye jar to her. Without thinking, Deborah caught it.

Alderman Harrison burst into the room. Behind him stood a mob of men in black coats, carrying torches. "Deborah Andersen?" he boomed.

"I have caught her!" Katherine shouted, pointing frantically at Deborah. "I have caught my evil daughter in the act of casting a spell!"

"Noooooo!" Deborah wailed. "It isn't true! Mother—tell them it isn't true!"

Harrison's eyes moved from the headless chicken on the floor, to the jar in Deborah's hand, to the blue dye covering her dress.

"Take her to the ship," he ordered.

The wooden farm wagon bounced over the rutted dirt road. Deborah sat propped on a pile of hay, her head knocking against the side of the wagon with each hard jolt.

Her arms were tied behind her back, underneath her blue cloak, and heavy iron chains bound her legs together.

They are carting me away like an animal to the slaughter, she thought bitterly.

The horse pulled the wagon slowly, groaning, its head down. Eight men in dark coats and high black hats marched alongside. Each carried a musket hoisted over his shoulder.

Even though the hour was late, villagers and farmers, many with torches, lined the road. They came to stare at the witch, to shout curses, and to throw eggs.

Deborah shut her eyes tightly so that she wouldn't see her neighbors' angry, twisted faces in the torchlight. Her eyes and cheeks were swollen from crying. Tears still streamed down her face, though she barely noticed them now.

An egg struck her shoulder and cracked, the yellow yolk dribbling down the front of her blue-stained dress. The horse whinnied and jerked the cart forward over a deep hole in the road.

Deborah's head slammed once again into the side of the wooden wagon. She moaned in pain and kept her eyes shut tight. If only she could sleep, escape this horror for a few minutes of peace. But the ugly shouts rang in her ears.

They reached the docks of Plymouth just after dawn.

The cart stopped in front of a two-masted ship, its sails tightly wrapped around the booms.

The ship bobbed gently in the water, straining against its ropes, the masts creaking and groaning.

From the wagon, Deborah watched the sailors in dark blue uniforms loading supplies into the cargo hold. They shouted to one another and laughed as they worked.

None of them turned to look at her.

The men who'd been guarding her dragged her roughly from the wagon. They loosened the chains at her feet so she could walk. But they didn't untie her hands.

Her legs trembled as the men guided her up the gangplank and onto the ship's deck. Her stomach churned with hunger. Her face burned from the salty tears she had shed all night long.

The ocean stretched darkly in front of her, reflecting the gray sky. Seabirds squawked, soaring against the gathering clouds.

A pale moon still floated over the water, even though a red morning sun was starting to rise.

The deck tilted beneath her feet. Deborah struggled not to fall. She had never been on a ship before.

Someone shoved her hard from behind, sending her stumbling to the rail. "Good riddance to the witch," one of the guards from her village muttered.

The guards turned and marched off the ship. Deborah shivered in her blue cloak.

Four red-faced sailors surrounded her and led her belowdecks. Deborah shyly glanced up at their faces, but none of them would look at her as they led her to a small, bare cabin.

Deborah saw a narrow bunk. A low table. A wooden chair. A tiny round porthole in the wall, looking out to sea.

The sailors untied her hands. Her wrists throbbed and ached. She tried to shake the numbness from her fingers.

One of the sailors handed her a bowl of warm porridge. She raised it gratefully to her face and inhaled the wheaty aroma. She hadn't eaten in over a day and was feeling faint from hunger.

"Thank you," she muttered. She began to spoon the porridge hungrily into her mouth.

The sailors still looked away from her. "We sail

tomorrow at dawn," one of them said.

And then they were gone.

She heard an iron bolt slide across the door and knew she had been locked inside.

She scraped the bowl of porridge clean and set it on the table. Then she tossed her blue cloak onto the bunk and dropped on top of it. The cabin swayed beneath her, a slow, steady rocking. The ship smelled of mildew and wood rot.

Deborah buried her head in her hands. I have done nothing to deserve this fate, she thought. She threw herself facedown on the bunk, and the tears began to flow again.

She lay on the bunk, crying, for hours, until at last she fell asleep. The door burst open, waking her. She had no idea how much time had passed.

Two sailors stepped into the cabin. They set a plate on the table, took the bowl with its crusted bits of dried porridge, and left, bolting the door behind them. Deborah sat up and studied the brown lumps on the plate—salty meat she didn't recognize, and a small, round lump of a potato.

The cabin swayed up and down. Have we set sail yet? she wondered. She peered through the porthole. She saw sailors gathered on the dock, laughing and shouting. No, the ship was still anchored in the port.

The muffled footsteps and shouts of the sailors rang out on the deck above her. As she ate the putrid food, she thought she heard the melody of a sailor's hornpipe. Or was it just the wind through the sails?

How long will I be sailing? she wondered. Where am I sailing to?

She had a hundred questions she would have liked to ask the sailors. But she knew they wouldn't answer. They wouldn't even look at her.

She returned to the bunk and closed her eyes. She didn't know whether she slept or not.

But she sat up when she heard heavy footsteps stomping on the lower deck. Footsteps approaching rapidly.

Are they bringing another meal? she wondered. Has that much time passed already?

She heard the bolt slide across the door.

The cabin door burst open.

A woman in a black cloak stepped inside. Her face was pale beneath her black hood.

Deborah uttered a cry of shock. "Mother!" she gasped. "What are *you* doing here?"

The cabin door closed. Deborah heard the bolt drop into place.

Katherine tossed her bag down. She wrapped her cloak around her and pulled the hood over her face until she was nearly hidden behind it.

Why has she followed me here? Deborah wondered, her pulse racing. Perhaps she will rescue me!

With a sigh, Katherine lowered herself into the small wooden chair. "They forced me to come," she said in a weary, hoarse voice. "I thought I was rid of you."

Deborah's heart sank. Of course her mother hadn't come to save her.

Katherine scowled at her daughter. "No ship captain would take you unless I agreed to go along. They said they needed me to keep your powers under control."

Deborah uttered a bitter laugh. "You know I have no powers. You are the evil one—not I."

And then Deborah's voice broke and a sob escaped her throat. "I don't understand, Mother. Why did you make the villagers hate me? Why did you make them think I was a witch?"

Katherine stared straight ahead, as if gazing right through her daughter. She didn't reply.

"Why?" Deborah demanded. "My entire life I was blamed for the spells you cast. How could you do that to me? I thought you were the only person in the world who loved me!"

Katherine's icy expression didn't change. "I couldn't let them suspect *me*—could I?" she said finally.

And then she added through gritted teeth, "I never wanted you. Never. But since I had you, I decided to make you useful."

The words stung Deborah. But they were so cold, so shocking, she didn't react at all. She stared blankly at her mother, her heart pounding in her chest.

"Those villagers were as stupid as cows," Katherine continued, spitting out the words. "I hated them! They all thought they were better than I. But I showed them for the fools they are. I made them pay for looking down at me—and they never guessed who was behind all their bad luck."

Deborah felt a dry sob heave in her chest. She had no tears left. "You had a daughter to take the blame."

Katherine nodded. "A daughter born with a blue

crescent moon on her temple. That made it so easy. So easy to make the villagers believe you were the evil one."

She isn't even sorry, Deborah thought, staring at her mother's stony face. She is smiling. She is *pleased* with herself!

Deborah turned her face away. She couldn't bear to look at her mother any longer. She curled up on the hard bunk, forcing herself not to cry.

I've cried my last tears, she thought angrily.

That woman is too evil to cry over.

Am I the most miserable girl in the world?

I must be, Deborah decided. I must be. . . .

Locked together in the cabin for the long sea journey, Deborah and her mother never spoke to each other. Deborah kept her gaze on the floor and tried to pretend that Katherine wasn't there.

During the day, Katherine read an old book she had brought. Deborah had always thought it was a prayer book. But now she realized it was full of curses and spells. At night Katherine slept with the book in her arms.

The sailors who brought their food spoke only to Katherine. When Deborah tried to ask them questions about the journey, they looked away and didn't reply.

They are terrified of me, Deborah realized.

They really believe my mother is keeping me from using my powers on them.

On the third week out from Plymouth, the ship ran into a storm. Thunder roared outside as the ship tossed on the sea. Rain pounded on the deck above and leaked through the seam of the porthole.

For hours the small cabin rocked and tilted. Deborah clung to the bunk, but the force of the wind bounced her and her mother from wall to wall. The table and chair overturned, sliding back and forth across the floor as the ship rocked. Deborah felt sick, but she forced herself not to show it.

She vowed she would never look weak in front of her mother again.

Never.

A few days after the storm ended, Deborah lay on the bunk, staring numbly at the ceiling. She heard heavy footsteps outside the cabin. And then the door sprang open.

Six blue-uniformed sailors appeared. "We have reached the island," one of them announced to Katherine. "Come with us. Take your daughter on deck. We will deliver her to shore."

"And then we shall set sail immediately back to England?" Katherine asked.

The sailor nodded. "Yes. Once your daughter is safely on shore."

Deborah's throat tightened. Her whole body tensed.

This is the moment, she thought. *This is the end of the journey.*

"We must hurry," the sailor told Katherine. "The

captain is eager to have the girl and her bad luck off the ship."

"Give me time to put on my cloak," Deborah said.

The sailors ignored her, as always.

Deborah turned and carefully unfolded the blue cloak she had kept at the foot of her bunk. She pulled it on loosely and slid the blue hood over her head.

Katherine stood ready in her black cloak. "That hood will not protect you from the lonely life that awaits you," she sneered.

"Mother, your cruelty will be rewarded," Deborah whispered.

Katherine uttered a cold, scornful laugh.

The sailors ushered them onto the deck. Deborah blinked in the bright sunlight. Then she gazed at the island, its sandy shore shimmering under the hot sun.

What are those strange trees? she wondered as she stared at the tall, bare trunks topped with long, lacy fronds. She'd never felt the sun shine so hot before, or so brightly. The water around her sparkled, clear and blue-green.

A sailor interrupted her thoughts. "We will take your daughter to shore on that skiff," he told Katherine, pointing to a small rowboat. "You may remain here."

Katherine nodded. "Good-bye, daughter," she said to Deborah with no feeling at all. Under the black hood, her face was a blank.

Walking stiffly, alert for trouble, the sailors surrounded Deborah. Two of them gripped her arms tightly and forced her toward the little boat.

Suddenly, Deborah felt one of the sailors let go of her arm. "My EYES!" he screamed.

"Owww. My eyes!" another sailor howled.

"I—I can't see!"

All along the vast deck, sailors screamed, howled in pain, and rubbed their eyes.

"I—I'm blind!"

"Help me! I can't see!"

"What kind of evil magic is this? We have all gone blind!"

As the blind sailors screamed and wailed in terror, Deborah turned to her mother.

Katherine's eyes narrowed on Deborah. She flung the black cloak to the deck and tensed her entire body, as if expecting a fight.

Deborah caught a flash of fear in her mother's eyes.

Katherine's chin trembled. She clenched her hands into fists.

It was the daughter's turn to smile.

"Do you wonder what is happening to these poor men, Mother?" Deborah asked. "At night when you slept, I slid your book from your arms. It was a long sea journey. Time enough for me to learn a few things."

"No!" Katherine gasped.

"I am not going to that island," Deborah said, pointing over the rail. "The *real* witch will be spending her life there—not I!"

Katherine sucked in a deep breath. "Foolish girl!"

she screamed. She raised her right hand, preparing to cast a spell on her daughter.

But Deborah acted quickly.

She slapped her mother's hand away. Then she shouted out the strange words she had taught herself from the old spell book.

Katherine froze like a statue.

Her eyes bulged. Her mouth gaped open. One arm was flung back. The other hand pointed at Deborah.

All around, the sailors wailed and screamed. Hands over their eyes, they staggered blindly around the deck.

Deborah acted quickly.

She knew the spell wouldn't keep her mother frozen for long.

She pulled off her blue cloak and swung it over Katherine's shoulders. She laced it tightly with trembling fingers, dropping the hood over Katherine's head.

Then Deborah shouted out another spell, a spell of strength.

She wrapped her arms around her mother's waist and lifted her up.

Staggering under the weight, Deborah made her way to the rail and raised Katherine's stiff body high.

"Good-bye, Mother," she said softly. "Have a wonderful life on the island."

Then she heaved Katherine over the rail.

Deborah watched her mother splash into the gentle waves. The blue cloak bubbled around Katherine as her body plunged into the water.

And then Deborah heard a sharp *cracking* sound as Katherine floated to the surface. The cracking spread, echoing over the ocean like thunder.

Deborah stared in amazement as the warm waters turned to ice.

The waves had been washing toward shore so gently. But now they creaked and cracked and froze in place.

Katherine bobbed in a large block of ice, surrounded by the frozen sea.

Leaning over the rail, Deborah saw her mother come out of the spell. Katherine blinked her eyes, staring through the ice. She shook her head. Moved her arms. Struggled to breathe.

She pounded on the ice, but she couldn't break through. Her skin was bright blue now, as blue as the frozen ocean. Gasping for breath, she raised a fist to the ship and shook it furiously at Deborah.

Over the cries of the blind sailors and the cracking of the ice, Katherine's angry words floated up to Deborah. "You and I will meet again, daughter!"

Then, quickly, the ice began to melt. The waves began to wash to shore again.

And, carried by the current, the block of ice with Katherine inside bobbed its way toward the island, where the shore was covered in smooth rocks.

Deborah watched the block of ice melt. She watched Katherine crawl out of the ocean onto the rocks, the blue cloak clinging to her back. Then Deborah turned away. It was the last she ever saw of her mother.

Ignoring the screaming sailors, Deborah strode across the deck to where Katherine's black cloak lay. She bent down and picked it up. She pulled it over her shoulders and hid her face inside the hood.

Then she uttered the words needed to return the sailors' sight to them.

Over the happy cries and cheers of the sailors, Deborah called out, "My daughter cast a spell on you. But nothing could keep her from the fate she deserved. Look—see her on the island. We can return home safely now."

She tried her best to sound like her mother. The sailors were so happy to have their sight back, they didn't question her.

Deborah pulled her hood over the blue crescent

moon on her temple, making sure it was well covered.

Two of the sailors guided her back to the cabin belowdecks. This time, they did not bolt the door.

I am going home to England, Deborah thought with a sigh. But what can I do there? Where can I go?

I cannot return to the village. That is certain.

She clutched the spell book to her chest.

Wherever I go, she thought, I will have to use the magic. I have no choice. I will have to use the powers.

On the island, Katherine watched the ship sail away. She watched until it disappeared over the horizon, seeming to fall off the earth.

Her hair was still wet. Small chunks of ice still clung to her skirt.

She spread the cloak out to dry. As she did so, the smooth gray rocks turned blue.

"You have not defeated me, Deborah!" she shouted, shaking her fist at the ocean. Seagulls took off, startled by the fury of her voice.

"You have not defeated me," Katherine cried. "I will stay alive here. I will take the breath—the very life of everyone unfortunate enough to stray onto this island. Their breath will keep me alive forever! And then I will take my vengeance on you, my daughter. Yes, someday . . . someday I will have my revenge!"

Part Three

The Present

September

"The island was wonderful," April said. "It really was a paradise." She smiled into the TV camera.

The interviewer, a young newsman named Jimmy Clark, pulled the microphone to his own mouth. "And the money you won? What did you have to do to win that money, April?"

April squinted into the studio lights. He poked the mike back into her face.

"We were divided into teams," April said. "And we had these contests called Life Games. And my team won the final contest, which was for bravery. So . . ."

"I'll bet you all were *very* brave to win a hundred grand!" Clark cut in. He laughed. "How did you win the bravery contest, April?"

April thought hard. "Uh . . . well . . ."

Why couldn't she remember?

She had been trying to remember some things about the island ever since she returned home. She could remember being abandoned by Marks and the others. She could remember nearly drowning trying to escape in that little boat.

She could remember saving Anthony's life. Marlin disappearing. Marlin's broken ribs.

But—*then* what happened?

How *did* her team win the bravery competition?

For some reason, that part seemed to be lost behind a fog.

"What was the most dangerous thing that happened?" her friend Pam Largent had asked when April returned home.

April had stared at Pam, thinking hard. "The most dangerous?"

Why couldn't she remember?

She pictured blue rocks. A cave cut into the rocks. She remembered a smell, a horrible odor.

But why couldn't she remember what happened at that cave?

And now, Jimmy Clark, the TV reporter, gazed at her eagerly, waiting for her answer.

"We all had to cross a rope bridge," April told him. "It was torn and broken, and a lot of the ropes were missing. If we fell, it would be a plunge straight down onto jagged rocks. I guess our team was the bravest on the bridge."

April knew that was a lie.

The rope bridge wasn't part of the bravery contest at all. But she just couldn't remember.

Had it been *too* frightening? Is that why April had shut it from her mind?

"Well, congrats again," Clark said, shaking hands with her. "And thanks for talking with us. I know you're going to be doing a lot of interviews. One last question—how does it feel to be a national celebrity?"

Is that what I am? April thought. Because I survived that island? I'm a national celebrity?

"Uh . . . it feels great!" she answered.

Pam was waiting for April when she got home. "You were awesome on TV!" she exclaimed, running up and hugging April. "Totally awesome!"

Whoa, April thought. What's this about? Pam and I have never been close friends. Why is she suddenly hugging me and telling me how great I am?

Pam was very tall and very blond and very pretty, with round blue eyes and a great smile. The girls' parents were best friends. So Pam and April were thrown together often, even though they didn't like each other very much.

When April was selected by The Academy to go to the island, Pam erupted in jealousy. "My grades are better, and I'm better at sports!" Pam had cried. She didn't try to hide her jealousy at all.

But ever since April had returned, Pam had been acting like her best pal.

Why is she doing it? April wondered. Then she scolded herself. I should be grateful that Pam has a new attitude.

"You're the most famous person Applegate Junior High ever had!" Pam gushed. She followed April to her room. "I can't believe you're my friend!"

Now she is overdoing it! April thought. *Pam wants something from me. I know she does.*

But what?

"When is your next interview? How many interviews are you doing? Are you going to say yes to that interview on MTV?" Pam bombarded April with questions.

"It's so totally exciting!" Pam exclaimed, not giving April a chance to answer.

"I know. I'm really lucky," April agreed. She sat down at her dressing table and began fiddling with her hair.

"Let me help you," Pam said, pulling a chair up beside her. "I have some great ideas for your hair. And for some cool things you can wear to your next interviews. What if we pulled your hair up this way and then tied it back here?"

April gazed at herself in the mirror as Pam restyled her hair. "Hey, that's good."

Pam really knows a lot about style. A lot more than I do, April thought with a frown.

"I saw some things at Urban Outfitters that would be totally cool," Pam said. "Especially if you do the MTV interview."

Pam stopped and stared at April's reflection. "And are you going to do the *Today* show?"

"Maybe," April said. "My parents still haven't decided if they want me to go to New York." She sighed. "The problem is, I'm missing so much school."

"Who *cares* about stupid school?" Pam cried. "You're a *star*!"

She brushed April's hair back from her forehead—and then gasped. "April—I don't believe it! You got a tattoo?"

"Huh?" April gazed into the mirror. She saw Pam's eyes on the blue crescent moon on her temple.

A chill ran down April's back.

Ever since she had returned home, the blue moon had been throbbing, throbbing. . . .

She jumped up from the dressing table. "It . . . it's not a tattoo," she said, covering the blue crescent with her hair. "It's a birthmark, I guess."

Pam narrowed her eyes at her. "Did you have it before?"

"Of course," April lied.

"It's kind of cool," Pam said, still studying April. "It really looks like a tattoo."

It isn't cool at all, April thought bitterly.

I don't know what it is or how it got there.

April sighed again. This is supposed to be the most exciting time in my life, she thought. So why do I feel so strange? Why do I feel as if I've forgotten something important?

Something terrible happened on that island, April told herself. Something so terrifying, I've shut away the memory.

"Wouldn't you love to go back to that island?" Pam asked. "Wouldn't you love to have a few more weeks there?"

April sighed. "It was great that my team won all that money," she told Pam. "But I'd never go back there. Never."

The next day, she received an invitation to return.

After school the next day, April was interviewed by some kids from her school newspaper. Then she hurried home because she had a ton of homework.

She walked in the door a little before five. "Anyone home?" she shouted, tossing down her bag.

To her surprise, she heard a dog barking. Alfy, Pam's enormous sheepdog, came bouncing across the living room, wagging his tail furiously.

Before April could move, the big dog jumped on her, shoving her against the wall with his big paws. Taking little jumps, Alfy stretched up his head, trying to lick her face.

"Down, boy," April said, laughing. "Thanks for the nice greeting. But get down!"

"Alfy—stop!" Pam came trotting into the room. She wrapped both hands around Alfy's collar and tugged the big, friendly sheepdog away from April. "He's too friendly. Too friendly!" she groaned.

April wiped dog drool off the front of her tank top.

"I was worried about you!" Pam said. "How come you're so late?"

"Worried about me?" April replied. "I had an interview, that's all."

What's the big deal? April thought. What is Pam's problem?

"What's up?" she asked. "What are you and Alfy doing here?"

Pam picked up a sandwich she'd been eating from the coffee table in front of the couch. "What do you mean? Didn't your parents tell you I'm living here?"

April's mouth dropped open. "Living here?"

Pam nodded, grinning. "For a whole month. They must have told you. My parents are off to Ghana for a month. And they set it up with your parents that Alfy and I could stay here."

April gaped at her. "It's been so crazy around here," she said. "I guess they forgot to tell me."

A feeling of dread swept over April. A whole month of seeing Pam night and day? Whoa.

At least they had a guest room. April wouldn't have to share her room. But did she need Pam living with her? No way.

"This is going to be so totally cool!" Pam gushed. "I know you and I haven't exactly been pals, April. But this will give us a chance to really get to know each other—right? We'll be like sisters!"

She hugged April again.

This can't be happening, April thought. Pam and me—sisters?

She pulled free of Pam and made her way to the stairs. "I've got to do some homework," she said. "I'm so far behind."

"If there's anything I can do to help, let me know," Pam called after her.

Did I remember to bring the short-story book home? April wondered as she climbed the stairs. She was still thinking about it as she stepped into her room—and uttered a low groan.

What was that odor? Rotten eggs?

"Ohhh." April pinched her fingers over her nose. But she couldn't shut the foul aroma out.

It swept over her, heavy and sour.

What *is* it? It smelled like fish. Like rotting meat. Like something decaying, something dead.

As the putrid odor washed over her, April started to choke.

Can't breathe, she thought. Can't breathe.

It's . . . suffocating me!

Gagging, tears pouring from her eyes, April staggered back through the bedroom doorway.

The sick odor followed her into the hall.

She started to gag. Her stomach lurched, and she swallowed hard, trying to force her lunch back down.

I know this smell, April thought.

A memory flashed into her mind. A vision of herself on the island. Entering the blue rock caves. Inhaling a disgusting smell.

April gasped. The smell was from the island. From those frightening caves.

How did it get here? How did it get in my room?

"Hey, what's wrong?" Pam stepped up behind her. "You look sick."

And then Pam's face twisted in disgust. "Yuck! Something stinks!"

Holding her nose, Pam stepped into April's bedroom. "What smells so bad? Did that bad dog Alfy have an accident in here?"

Swallowing hard, April followed Pam into the room. "I—I've got to open a window," she choked out.

Halfway across the room, she stopped when she saw the bones on the rug beside her bed.

White bones of a small animal. Piled in a perfect circle.

Another memory jolted April. Climbing, exploring a dark cave. Looking down. Seeing a circle of white bones.

Just like on the island! April remembered. Just like the bones outside that rock cave!

Staring at the bones, inhaling the stench from the rock cave on the island, April couldn't control herself any longer.

She opened her mouth in a shrill scream of horror.

"April—what is it? April—please stop!" Pam grabbed April by the shoulders. "Stop!"

Something horrible happened on the island, April told herself, staring at the pile of bones. And now it has followed me home!

She heard footsteps in the hall. Her mom and dad burst into the doorway. "What's going on?" Mr. Powers asked.

"The bones—" April pointed.

Pam stepped in front of her. "I'm really sorry," she said to April's parents. "Alfy is always dragging things into the house. For some reason, those bones upset April."

"It—it's the *smell* too!" April cried, trembling.

"Smell?" Mrs. Powers sniffed loudly. "What smell?"

All four of them sniffed.

"It's . . . gone," April murmured.

Pam bent down and started to collect the bones. "I'll get these out of here right away," she said. "Alfy thought he was bringing you a present."

April realized her parents were staring at her. "All the excitement has made you a little tense, hasn't it?" her mother said softly.

April nodded. "I guess."

"I know you've been having nightmares about the island. Maybe we should cancel some of the interviews you have scheduled," Mr. Powers suggested.

"Maybe," April said. She tried to force the pile of bones from her mind.

"Oh. I almost forgot. You have mail," Mrs. Powers said. She handed April a square cream-colored envelope. "From The Academy."

April stared at the envelope in her hands. "What could it be? It looks kind of like an invitation."

Mrs. Powers laughed. "Well, you'll never know unless you open it."

"Yes, open it," Pam said eagerly, peering over April's shoulder.

April carefully pulled open the envelope. Then she unfolded the note inside.

"It *is* an invitation," she said.

"To what?" Pam asked.

"A reunion," April said, her eyes scanning the letter. She gazed up at her mother. "Donald Marks is having a reunion of all the kids from the island."

"A reunion? When?" Mrs. Powers asked.

"In two weeks," April said, reading. "On the island. It says they'll fly me there for free."

"Whoa! That's totally cool!" Pam exclaimed.

"It says it's going to be taped for TV. And . . . it's a chance for everyone to get together one more time to celebrate the fun we had."

"Wow. That's awesome," Pam said. Then her expression changed. "But you said you didn't want to go back there, didn't you? You know what? If you'd like, I'd be willing to go in your place."

April looked up from the invitation and glared at Pam. "Go in my place?"

"Of *course* April wants to go," Mrs. Powers broke in. "But it does seem a shame to leave Pam here by herself. Maybe Pam could go to the reunion too."

Pam's eyes grew wide. "Do you really think so?"

"I'll bet Marks wouldn't mind," April's mom said. "Why don't I call and ask? There's a phone number on the invitation—right?"

"Yes, but—" April started to say.

Why on earth did Mom suggest that? April asked herself angrily. This is why Pam has been so nice to me. She was so jealous that I got to go to the island. Now she wants to horn in on it.

"Uh . . . Pam is right. I don't think I want to go," April said, keeping her eyes on the invitation.

"April, you have to go," Mrs. Powers said sternly. "You're one of the grand prize winners—remember? You have to be there. You can't disappoint everyone."

"And you want to be on TV—right?" Pam chimed in.

April opened her mouth to protest.

But her mom pulled the invitation from her hand. Then she turned and hurried out of the room. "I'm going to call Marks right now and see if Pam can go too."

"Wow! Thanks!" Pam said excitedly. "That would be so totally cool!" She flashed April a big grin, then followed Mrs. Powers downstairs.

April dropped onto the edge of her bed with a sigh. She stared down at the pile of bones on the carpet.

Pam was so excited about going to the island with me, she forgot about the bones, April realized.

She pictured the rock cave again.

Something terrifying happened there, April thought.

I don't want to go back. I really don't want to go back.

It had rained all afternoon, and the street was puddled with deep circles of water. Reflecting the moonlight, the puddles glowed like spotlights.

Down the block, the clock in the library tower chimed midnight. A van filled with teenagers roared past April. Its tires splashed a wave of water over her. "Get out of the street!" a boy yelled from the back of the van.

Startled, she cried out and jumped to the curb.

Her bare feet sank into the soft mud at the side of the road. She shivered and pulled her hair back with both hands.

Another car sped closer. The headlights rolled over April. She covered her eyes from the bright light and kept walking.

Trees showered cold rainwater down on her head. She shivered again as she crossed the street. The pavement felt cold and rough under her feet.

The street was deserted now. Down the block a traffic light changed from red to green.

Green for go, April thought.

I'm going. I'm going—where?

Moving away from the street into the darkness of the trees, April hoisted herself onto the low stone wall that bordered Franklin Park. When we were little, my friends and I played in this park every day, she remembered.

She crossed the playground, moving behind the long row of swings. She pushed each swing until she had set them all in motion.

A gust of wind rustled the trees. April searched for swaying palm trees.

"But there are no palm trees in Ohio," she told herself in a whisper.

She trotted over the grass, past the softball diamond. Blades of grass stuck wetly to the soles of her feet.

The stone climbing-hill gleamed like ivory under the bright moonlight. I haven't climbed this hill since I was six, April thought.

She gazed up at the small black cave-hole cut into the top of the hill. Yes! You slip into that cave opening up there and then there's a slide that takes you down to the bottom of the hill, she remembered.

She lowered herself onto her hands and knees and climbed onto the hill. The stones, still damp from the afternoon rain, felt smooth and cold.

"YAAAAAAY!" A happy, childlike cry escaped her throat. She started to climb up the hill.

This seemed so high and steep to me when I was a kid, April thought. But it's totally babyish. I'm nearly to the top.

She reached a hand up to grab the bottom of the cave opening—and pulled herself into the round black hole.

Into the cave, she thought.

Into the stone cave . . . into the blackness.

She hesitated. It's going to carry me away. If I go inside, I will fall forever.

I will fall through the darkness and never be seen again.

The wind blew into the hole, making a dull whistling sound.

April realized her whole body was shaking. "Please—please don't make me go in the cave!" she begged.

Then she saw the flashing red light.

At first, she thought it was a burning torch.

Who is carrying a torch through the forest? she wondered. Is it someone on my team?

And then she saw the black-and-white patrol car on the other side of the low wall. The light on top of the car flashed red-blue, red-blue, red-blue.

Two dark-uniformed officers jumped the wall and were jogging through the playground toward April.

"Hey!" one of them called to her. He was very young, she saw, with tiny, dark eyes and the shadow of a black mustache.

"What are you doing up there?" his partner, a woman officer, shouted.

"Climbing!" April called back.

The two officers stopped beneath April at the bottom of the hill. Beneath their caps, they frowned at her. "It's late," the woman said softly. "The park is closed."

April squinted down at them, suddenly dizzy.

"Why are you here?" the officer asked again.

The words rang in April's ears. "Why am I climbing this hill to the cave?" she asked out loud.

She uttered a gasp. "I don't know."

"You're in your pajamas," the woman officer said. "And you're barefoot."

April gazed down at her red-and-white-striped pajamas. I'm out in my pajamas? But—why? she asked herself.

"I—I thought I was home in bed," she told the officers. "I—I didn't know . . . "

And then she glimpsed a figure, half hidden by the side of the patrol car.

Pam!

"Pam—what are you doing here?" April called in a trembling voice.

Pam took a few steps closer, her hands in her jacket pockets. Her blond hair fluttered in the wind.

"I—I followed you," Pam said. "I saw you go out, April. And I was so worried. So I followed you.

What are you doing out here? Why did you leave the house?"

"I don't know," April told her. "I don't know I don't know I don't know I don't know I don't know."

And then she was back on the island.

It had to be a dream, right? But why were the colors so vivid, everything so real, as if she could reach out and touch the trees, the sandy ground, the blue rocks?

She felt so hungry, her stomach gnawed. Too weak to walk, she crawled over the rocks. Her throat ached from dryness, as if she'd been eating sand.

I have to find food, she thought. I have to find food or I'll starve.

She picked up a small brown coconut off the ground. Yes! She pounded it against a tree trunk. Pounded it. Pounded it.

I'm too weak, she realized. Too weak to crack it open.

She stared at the coconut between her hands. She could practically taste the sweet milk inside, the chunky meat.

It's like the mystery I'm trying to solve, she thought as she dreamed. So close . . . I'm so close.

But I can't get to it. It's locked away from me.

Then Marlin appeared. He sat cross-legged in front of her.

How long had he been there?

His dark eyes reflected the moonlight. April saw two crescent moons in his eyes.

"Marlin—where have you been?" she asked.

"I disappeared," he answered in a low, flat voice that wasn't his.

"But where?" she asked.

"I disappeared here. On the island," he told her. "I am going to stay here forever."

April saw a flash of blue inside a cave. Was someone watching them?

"It's time for you to come home," she told Marlin.

"No. I disappeared here," he replied.

"You have to come home," April insisted. "You have to come home—now."

He gazed blankly at her. She could see the crescent moons in his eyes. But he had no expression now. No life.

"Come home, Marlin," she said.

She reached for him. Grabbed his arm and tugged.

And Marlin's arm came off in her hand.

It's stone, she realized. Blue stone.

And then Marlin's head rolled off his shoulders. The stone head dropped to the rocky ground and broke in half.

Marlin's other arm broke off. His whole body cracked into chunks of stone.

And April woke up screaming. Screaming again. Another nightmare about the island.

"You're up early," Mrs. Powers said. She stood at the sink, pouring herself a mug of coffee.

"Couldn't sleep," April muttered, yawning. "Another nightmare." She dropped onto a wooden stool at the kitchen counter.

"Your dad and I are terribly, terribly worried about you," Mrs. Powers said. She carried her coffee to the counter and perched next to April.

Mom looks more tired than usual, April thought. Dark circles around her eyes. April noticed strands of white running through her mother's wavy blond hair.

"That crazy thing you did last night," her mother said, studying her carefully.

She is studying me like one of her lab specimens, April thought. Mrs. Powers was a lab technician at an animal research lab.

"The police officers said you didn't remember going out in your pajamas like that. They said you couldn't answer their questions. You looked dazed."

April nodded sadly. "I wish I could explain."

"Thank goodness Pam followed you," her mother said. "At least you had a good friend watching out for you."

"Yeah," April muttered.

"It's so frightening. I'm going to make an appointment for you with Dr. Jackson," Mrs. Powers said. "You'll go after school."

She ran a hand tenderly through April's hair. "And we canceled your interview with that TV show for tonight. You're okay with that—right?"

"Fine," April whispered. She shut her eyes and saw Marlin's stony body cracking apart again.

"I know being on TV is a lot of fun for you," Mrs. Powers said, pouring April a glass of grape juice. "But maybe we should stop all the interviews for a while."

"Fine," April repeated.

Mrs. Powers shook her head. "You had such a fabulous, exciting time. I can't understand what's giving you bad dreams and making you do crazy things."

"I can't either," April said softly. She sipped the grape juice.

"Do you think you should stay home from school today?" her mother asked.

April shook her head. "No. I'll be fine. Really."

She glanced at the clock. "But it's so early, know what I'm going to do? I'm going for a jog before I get dressed for school."

"You sure?" her mother asked.

"Yeah. It will help clear my head," April said. "I always feel better after I run."

She changed into shorts, a tank top, and running shoes. Then she clipped her CD player to her waist, and headed back downstairs.

She bumped into Pam at the front door. Pam yawned. "I guess I overslept a little. Are you feeling okay? Going for a jog?"

April nodded.

"I was using your Discman yesterday. Hope you don't mind," Pam said. "I left a new CD in it for you. Totally awesome. Let me know if you like it."

April nodded again. She didn't feel like talking to Pam. She pushed open the door and stepped outside.

It was a bright fall morning. A red sun, just peeking over the trees, made the lawns shimmer like emeralds.

April did warm-up exercises for a few minutes in her driveway. Then she adjusted the headphones over her ears as she started to jog.

The Millers across the street waved to her as they climbed into their SUV to go to work. April turned the corner and picked up speed.

The morning air feels so fresh and cool, she thought.

She pushed Play on the disc player and fiddled with the volume dial as she ran.

Her running shoes thudded over the sidewalk. She could feel her leg muscles begin to loosen up.

When the music didn't start, she found the volume control again and turned it higher.

April heard singing. She listened for a few moments, jogging at a fast, steady pace.

What *is* this CD? she wondered.

And then she stopped with a gasp—and listened to the woman's voice coming through the headphones.

The same eerie voice she had heard on the island.

"No! No!" April cried. "Please, leave me alone!"

The woman's voice lingered in April's ears.

The same slow, sad song in that strange language. The same woman with her low, throaty voice.

"No! No! It can't be!" April wailed. "This can't be happening to me!"

She ripped the disc player from her waist and heaved it to the ground. Her legs were trembling too hard to jog.

She held on to a lamppost, struggling to calm her racing heart. Then she turned and began walking unsteadily home.

An hour later April stood in the front hall at school, arguing with Pam.

"Pam—I begged you to cancel the assembly!" April said. "I—I really don't want to talk about the island. You know that I—I—"

Pam rolled her eyes. "April, the whole school is waiting to hear you," she said.

She took April's hand and began tugging her to

the auditorium. "I went to so much trouble setting this up," Pam said. "I did this whole thing for *you*."

"But I—I just can't," April protested. "You know I've been having problems. And—"

Pam didn't seem to hear her. She tugged April to the auditorium.

I should have stayed home today, April thought. But I thought coming to school would take my mind off the island.

I completely forgot about the assembly Pam set up.

How can I do this? What if something terrible happens to me in front of the whole school?

"It will be easy," Pam said, holding open the auditorium door. "Just talk about what the games were like and what you did on the island. Then Mrs. Harper wants to give you some kind of medal or something."

She pushed April into the auditorium.

April swallowed hard as she saw that all the seats were filled. The whole school was there.

A man raised a camera as she walked in, then flashed her picture. Blinking from the sudden light, April followed Pam to the stage. Kids broke into applause as they saw her.

"Well, our special guest has arrived," Mrs. Harper, the junior high principal, announced, beaming. She motioned to April, and the applause grew even louder.

She was standing at a podium in the center of the stage. And surrounding her were four tall cardboard cutouts of palm trees.

"We even built a set for you this morning, April!" Mrs. Harper said. "To make you feel at home."

April stared at the brightly painted palm trees. A chill ran down her back. She took a deep breath and made her way across the stage to the podium.

"I think many of you know April Powers," Mrs. Harper said, leaning over the microphone. "Well, April recently returned from an exciting adventure on a tropical island. And this morning, we've asked her to tell you all about it."

Another round of applause as April stepped behind the podium. She felt a tingle of nervousness in her chest. Her mouth was suddenly dry.

But she was a good speaker. She didn't get stage fright.

She and Pam competed on the debate team to see who could speak the best. Of course, Pam had to win every competition. But April believed she was just as good a speaker.

Gripping the edges of the podium, she leaned forward and began to tell about her trip to the island. She started at the beginning, with the invitation letter she received from the organization called The Academy.

She told her audience about the boat ride to the island. About meeting Donald Marks, The Academy leader. About her teammates and the Life Games competition.

As she talked, April started to relax. It's going very well, she told herself. I think the kids are really enjoying my stories.

As she talked about the kayak race around the island, she glanced at the clock at the side of the stage. Have I really been talking for twenty minutes? she asked herself.

She took a long sip of water from the glass on the podium. "I guess the strangest thing about the island," she continued, "was the blue rocks. There were hills of these rocks. They were smooth and dark blue. And the strangest thing about them was they were always cold to the touch—even under the broiling hot sun.

"We had a rock-climbing contest on those rocks," April said. "A race up to the caves at the top. And I—"

April stopped when she heard the loud *chop*.

It seemed to have come from behind her.

She turned to the sound—and saw a chop mark in one of the cardboard palm trees.

Chop.

Another loud, cutting sound. This one to her right.

She spun to see that another tree had a cut in its trunk.

Chop. Chop.

Chop.

The frightening sound repeated.

"Just like that night!" she cried into the microphone. "Just like that night in the forest!"

April didn't want to look at the cardboard trees with their ugly chop marks.

She closed her eyes tightly—and a picture formed

in her mind. She could see herself on the island. She was walking through the woods with Kristen, Marlin and Anthony.

They were lost. Hopelessly lost. And then they heard it.

Chop.

Chop.

Chop.

The chopping sounds surrounded them. Echoed through the forest. Came at them from everywhere at once!

Chop.

Chop.

Chop.

"It—it's happening again!" April screamed.

She opened her eyes and saw Pam at the side of the stage, staring at her, mouth hanging open in shock. April saw the puzzled faces of kids in the audience.

I've got to try to continue, she thought. The whole school is watching me.

She cleared her throat. "A terrible storm came up," she began, shouting over the chopping sounds all around. "The storm came out of nowhere and—"

The stage lights flickered overhead.

Lightning! April thought.

Lightning overhead.

A dim, frightening memory floated at the edge of her mind.

I saw lightning flashing over someone. Someone

stood close to me—someone terrifying—and lightning flashed.

The stage lights flickered again.

April turned to the side of the stage—*and saw her*!

The woman! The woman in the blue cloak!

Running across the stage to capture her.

"Come with me!" the woman called. "April, come with me now!"

"THERE SHE IS! THERE SHE IS!" April shrieked into the microphone. She pointed with a trembling finger at the advancing woman.

"Now I remember!" April cried. "Now I remember everything!"

The auditorium rang out with startled cries as the stage lights exploded. Lights burst apart. Glass shattered and fell to the stage.

"Come with me, April!" the woman called.

"NOOOOO!" April wailed.

Kids screamed as April leaped off the stage.

She landed hard on the concrete floor. Her knees bent and she almost fell.

Pain shot up her legs. But she kept her balance and took off, running up the long auditorium aisle.

"Stop her!" Mrs. Harper was shouting from the stage.

But the startled kids in the audience didn't move. April ran up the aisle and out the door. Her heavy footsteps echoed in the empty front hall.

A secretary from Mrs. Harper's office called out to her. "April? What's wrong?"

April kept running. Out the front door. Into the bright, sun-drenched morning. Everything glowing. Gold and bright blue and green.

She ran into the colors.

Where was she running? She didn't know.

She wasn't thinking. She lost all sense of time, of where she was, of what was happening.

It was as if she were moving through a dream of bright, shimmering colors.

And then strong hands grabbed her from behind.

She's caught me! April thought.

April spun around. "Pam!"

"April—what happened? Where are you going?" Pam cried breathlessly.

"The chopping sounds—" April gasped, struggling to catch her breath.

Pam's face twisted in confusion. "The *what?*"

"The lightning—" April croaked.

"You mean the lights popping?" Pam asked. "Yeah. That was weird."

"And she was there, Pam," April said. "She was there. Running after me."

"You mean Mrs. Harper?" Pam asked, still holding on to April's shoulders. "Yes. I saw Mrs. Harper running across the stage to you. She thought you were having trouble."

"NO!" April protested. "It wasn't Mrs. Harper! It was the woman in the blue cloak. The woman from the cave who—"

"Calm down," Pam said gently. "Please. Let me take you back to school. Maybe the nurse—"

"No!" April tugged free of Pam. "I—I can't."

"You know, you probably shouldn't go back to the island," Pam said suddenly.

"Huh?"

"I'm really worried about you, April. I don't think you could handle the reunion. I think I should go in your place. I really do."

The two girls stared at each other, both breathing hard.

Finally, April spoke. "You're a real friend," she said bitterly.

Then she turned and ran.

"April—wait!"

She heard Pam's shout, but she didn't turn back. She ran back into the bright colors of the day. Floating over lawns and streets.

Where am I going? she asked herself. It's as if I'm being pulled . . . Pulled away from school. Pulled somewhere new. Pulled out of my own control.

At times she slowed to a walk to catch her breath. Then she would run again.

Not looking. Not seeing anything but the shifting colors. The clear sky above, clear as the ocean waters. The trees, waving in a soft wind like the palm trees on the island.

I'm not on the island, she told herself. I'm back home.

The island is thousands of miles away from here. Thousands . . .

So why am I running? Where am I going?

And then she heard a voice calling to her. A boy's voice, sounding very far away.

"April . . . April . . ." He called.

April stopped running. She glanced around. She didn't see anyone. "Who's there?"

"April . . . it's me!" the voice called.

"Huh? Marlin?" Again she gazed in a circle. "Where are you, Marlin?"

"Help me, April!" he called. So far away. His voice a whisper on the wind. "Come back for me. You have to come back for me!"

A chill prickled the back of April's neck. "Marlin? Come back? What do you mean?" she called shrilly. "Where are you? Marlin?"

Silence now.

April stood trembling, waiting for the voice to return.

Silence.

She leaned over, pressed her hands against her knees, and waited for her heartbeat to slow. Then she stood up and glanced around.

I'm at a mall, April realized. But which mall? I don't recognize it. This isn't the Applegate mall.

How did I get here? Why don't I remember?

Her throat ached. Her mouth was so dry, she couldn't swallow.

Across the aisle, two women with shopping carts

were staring at her.

I've been running so long, I must look horrible, April thought. She brushed back her hair with both hands and straightened her bangs. Or maybe those women are wondering why I'm not in school.

Well, I'm wondering too, she thought unhappily.

She wiped the sweat off her forehead with the back of her hand. A sign a few stores down caught her eye: YE OLDE ICE CREAM PARLOR.

I've got to get something to drink, April thought. She made her way into the small restaurant—all white, white as vanilla ice cream—white walls, white ceiling, white tables, and white booths.

She ordered a raspberry iced tea and a bottle of water. Then she started to carry her tray to a table.

But she stopped halfway across the restaurant—and stared at a girl sitting alone in the back booth.

I know that girl, she thought. She looks so familiar.

And then April screamed, "Kristen—what are *you* doing here?"

Kristen had an ice cream sundae in front of her. She dropped her spoon to the table, and her mouth opened in shock as April came hurrying over to her booth.

"April?" Kristen cried. "No way! I don't believe it!"

She jumped up, and the two girls hugged as if they were old friends.

"This is impossible!" April exclaimed. "Impossible! What are you doing here?"

"We don't have school today," Kristen explained. "My mom dropped me off here at the mall. I'm meeting some kids at the movie theater later."

April set her tray on the table and slid into the white booth across from Kristen. "But—but—" She felt too shocked to speak.

Kristen laughed. "Calm down. Look at you. You're drenched with sweat." She handed April a paper napkin. "What's your problem anyway?"

"I—I've been running," April replied. She mopped her forehead, then her cheeks. "But I don't believe you're here. I know you don't live in Applegate."

"Applegate?" Kristen squinted across the table at April. "You're kidding—right? This isn't Applegate. This is New Town Village." She picked up the spoon and took a chunk of chocolate ice cream.

April's mouth dropped open. She tried to say something, but only a squeak came out.

Kristen spooned up her sundae, staring hard at her, studying her.

"New Town Village?" April finally managed to speak. "But that's two towns away from Applegate."

Kristen nodded. "So?"

April felt panic tighten her throat. "I—I must have run all the way. I don't remember. I mean, that's so far. What time is it?"

Kristen glanced at her watch. "Two-fifteen. Hey—are you all right? Did you really run through two towns? Why? Why did you do it?"

April stared back at her, thinking hard.

Kristen reached across the table and squeezed April's hand. "April, you're shaking!"

"I don't know why I did it," April murmured. "I . . . I don't know."

And then the room began to spin in front of her. The white walls, the white floor, the white booths . . .

"April? Hey, April?" Kristen was squeezing her hand. "What's up with you?"

"I . . . don't know," April said. She took a long drink of the iced tea. "Everything is crazy, Kristen. Crazy and frightening. Did you get your invitation to the reunion?"

Kristen nodded. "Are you going?"

"I really don't want to," April replied. "Since we got back from the island, the strangest things have been happening to me."

Kristen spooned up the last of the chocolate syrup in her sundae bowl. She set the spoon down and gazed hard at April. "Strange things? Like what?"

And then it all burst from April in a breathless stream of words.

She told Kristen about that morning—the chopping sound behind the cardboard trees, and the lightning, and the woman in the blue cloak on the stage. And about the woman singing in her headphones. And hearing Marlin call to her for help. And the night the police found her on the playground rock hill.

When she finally finished, her heart was pounding. April gulped down the iced tea.

"You think I'm crazy—don't you?" she said, returning Kristen's stare. "You think I've totally lost it."

"No way," Kristen said softly. Her expression grew solemn. "The same things have been happening to me."

“Wow,” April murmured. “Are you serious?”

Kristen nodded. “Yes. The same things. It’s as if . . . something followed me back from the island. Something won’t let me get back to my normal life.”

“That’s just how I feel!” April exclaimed. “But I thought it was only me. Oh, I’m so glad I ran into you. You’ve made me feel so much better.”

“Me too,” Kristen said.

“What about the others?” April wondered. “Do you think these frightening things are happening to them too? Have you heard from anyone else?”

Kristen nodded. “I got an e-mail from Anthony a week or so ago,” she replied. “He said everything was great. He loves all the TV interviews and attention he’s been getting. He didn’t mention anything weird going on.”

“What about Marlin?” April asked.

“I haven’t heard from him,” Kristen said.

“I haven’t either,” April said. “And he promised that he’d write to me.”

She grabbed Kristen's hand. "Do you remember the woman in the blue cloak? The woman by the rock caves? I didn't make her up—did I?"

"I remember her," Kristen replied softly. "I remember her, April. I tried to rescue you from her. Oh, yes. I remember. How could I forget her?"

"Well . . . what if she's the one who's been doing these things to us?" April asked, her voice shaking. "What if she hypnotized us or something? And that's why these weird things are happening to us. What if she has Marlin? What if she's captured him and kept him on the island?"

"Whoa," Kristen murmured. "Take it easy. That's crazy! Marks told us that Marlin was okay—remember? He told us that Marlin was being flown home."

"But what if Marks lied?" April asked. "After Marlin disappeared, we never saw him again."

"I'm sure he's home and he's fine," Kristen replied. She rummaged in her bag and pulled out a cell phone. "Let's call Marlin right now."

"You have his number?" April asked.

Kristen nodded.

She searched the bag till she found a tiny scrap of paper. "Here it is. Let's just call Marlin and ask him what's going on with him."

She handed the phone to April. "You do it. You were his pal."

Kristen read off the phone number, and April pushed the buttons. She pressed the little phone tightly to her ear and listened.

Please pick up, Marlin, she thought. Please, please—be okay.

Please—let that voice on the wind be just my imagination.

But a woman answered the phone.

"Amanda Davis." She had a low, husky voice.

"Is this Marlin's mom?" April asked.

"Yes, it is," Mrs. Davis answered. "Who is calling, please?"

"Is Marlin there?" April asked. She crossed her fingers. "My name is April. I'm a friend of his."

"No, April. Marlin isn't home," Mrs. Davis replied. "Do you know about The Academy thing Marlin got into? On an island? He's still there. He'll be there another week or so."

April swallowed hard. A chill shook her body. "Thank you," she whispered.

She clicked off the phone. Then she turned back to Kristen. "Marlin never came home," she said softly.

Kristen's mouth dropped open. Her face turned pale. "I don't believe it," she whispered.

April took a long, shuddering breath. "We've got to go back there," she said. "We have no choice, Kristen. We've got to go back to that island and find him."

April had just enough money to take a taxi home. On the way, she decided what she had to do.

I'm going to call Donald Marks, she decided. I'm going to make him explain exactly what is going on.

She sneaked into her house through the back door. She didn't want to run into Pam.

In her room, she searched the desk until she found the original invitation from The Academy. Her eyes glanced over the bold black letterhead at the top of the letter.

Yes!

Here it is. The phone number of The Academy in New York City.

April picked up the phone. Downstairs, she could hear Pam telling Alfy to "sit, boy. Sit."

Mom and Dad won't be upset if I make a long distance call to New York, April decided. I mean, this is really important.

She stared at the phone number. If I tell Donald Marks all the weird things that have been happening, maybe he'll know why, she thought.

Maybe he can help me.

April's heart started to pound as she punched in the number and listened to the phone start to ring.

April listened to two rings . . . three.

Then a woman answered. "Good afternoon. The Academy. How can I direct your call?"

April told the woman who she was and asked to speak to Donald Marks.

After a long wait, he picked up the phone. "Hello, April. What a nice surprise. How are you doing? So nice to hear from you," he boomed.

"Hi. I . . . uh . . . I'm not doing so well," April started to say. "I wanted to ask you—"

"Your mother called me and asked if your friend could come along with you to the reunion," Marks cut in. "I said yes, of course. The more the merrier. Especially if she's a friend of one of our winners."

"Well, I didn't really call you about that," April said. She took a deep breath. "You see, Mr. Marks, some strange things—"

"I'm so excited you will be coming to the reunion," Marks interrupted again. "I have some amazing things planned. I can't believe we're all going back to that beautiful island so soon—can you?"

"No, I really can't," April said. "But the reason I'm calling—"

"And it's all going to be on TV," Marks said. "By the way, April, I've seen some of the TV interviews you've done. You are very good on camera. Have you ever thought of going into TV or performing when you are older?"

"No. Not really," April replied.

She squeezed the phone. Why won't he let me get a single word in?

"I hope you and your family are enjoying the money you won," Marks said. "Our time on the island was an amazing experience for everyone. I hope you're looking forward to the reunion, as I am."

April couldn't take it anymore. "I called to ask you about Marlin!" she screamed. "Why didn't Marlin come home? I talked to his mother and she said he was still on the island. So I was wondering—"

"Oh, sorry," Marks cut in. "I have another call. April, I have to get off. It was good to hear from you. I'll see you and your friend very soon at the reunion. Say hi to your mom for me."

The line went dead.

April sat with the phone pressed to her ear. He didn't listen to a word I said, she thought angrily.

Was he really that excited about the reunion? Or was he trying not to answer any of my questions?

I have to phone Kristen and tell her what happened.

April heard heavy footsteps in the hall. She turned, expecting to see Pam, but Alfy came lumbering into her room. His tail was waving furiously, and he bumped his big, furry head against her leg.

"Alfy—did you come up to visit me?" April said,

petting his head, running her fingers through his long, thick fur.

She climbed off her chair and dropped beside the dog on the rug. "You're such a friendly guy. Do you want to play? Is that what you want?"

Alfy bumped her again, as if saying yes.

April wrapped her arms around him. "You're just a big teddy bear, aren't you!" His fur felt so good, like a thick, warm shag rug.

She started to wrestle around with him playfully. She put him in a headlock and pulled him onto his back. Tail still wagging, the big dog kicked his paws in the air.

Then he flopped himself around—on top of April.

"Ow! You weigh a ton! Get off me, you big lug!" April cried, laughing.

The dog didn't budge. Instead, he turned and lowered his head to April's and sniffed her face.

"Get off! You're squishing me!" April exclaimed. She was laughing too hard to shove the dog away.

"Stop! Hey—stop!"

Alfy lowered his face and licked her cheek.

"Yuck!" April cried. "Gross!"

Alfy licked her cheek again. Then he pressed his snout to her mouth.

"Hey—no lips! No lips!" April pleaded.

To her surprise, the dog pressed down hard, pushing his wet snout to her mouth.

April stopped laughing.

What is this big goof doing? she wondered.

And then she felt the dog take a strong, powerful breath.

"Hey!"

She shoved hard with both hands, trying to push Alfy away.

But he didn't budge. He pressed his open mouth against hers—and inhaled.

April felt her breath being sucked out.

Noooooo! She tried to call out—but the dog smothered her voice. His head pressed over her face, heavy as a bowling ball.

Alfy sucked in another deep breath. And another.

Help! Oh, help! April thought.

I can't move him. I can't stop him.

He's sucking my breath out. Sucking my *life* out.

Like the woman in the blue cloak. Like the woman on the island.

This is crazy! Why is this happening?

Oh . . . help.

"What's going on in here?" a voice called.

Pam burst into the room, followed by April's mom.

Thank goodness, April thought. I'm rescued.

Mrs. Powers let out a startled cry. "You're wrestling with the dog? Is that what all the bumping and thumping was?"

Alfy licked April's cheeks.

"Pam and I thought the ceiling was about to fall in!" Mrs. Powers declared. "And you were just playing—"

"You don't understand," April broke in.

She struggled to push the big sheepdog away. But he hovered over her, licking her face playfully.

"Alfy . . . he . . . he . . . " She felt too weak to talk.

"Alfy loves to wrestle," Pam said. "And he loves to lick." She laughed. "Your face is a sticky mess, April."

"You . . . you don't understand," April stammered. "He wasn't playing. He . . . "

"The big goof just doesn't realize that he's part

elephant!" Pam said. She pulled Alfy away from April and gave the dog a hug.

April stared up at Pam. She felt a chill at the back of her neck.

It's weird, she thought. Every time one of these frightening things happens to me, Pam is there.

Pam is always there.

April and Pam flew to Los Angeles. From there, they would fly to the main island. Then they would take a boat to the tiny island to join Marks and the others.

On the flight to Los Angeles, Pam chattered the whole way. April tuned her out and thought about the reunion.

She couldn't wait to see the other kids. She was dying to ask them if strange things had been happening to them too.

And she was eager to solve the mystery about Marlin.

Kristen was right, April decided. We *had* to come to this reunion.

The boat rocked gently in the sparkling ocean waters. The bright sun made the waves shimmer like gold.

At the pier, there had been lots of hugs and happy cries as the kids all greeted one another.

Even that sourpuss Anthony is cheerful today, April thought. Everyone is so excited about being on TV.

She searched for Donald Marks, but he was nowhere to be seen. Pam was busy introducing herself to everyone and chatting everyone up.

It was a beautiful summer day, but April felt cold and frightened. As the island came into view, she stared at the strange blue rocks—and felt a shiver of dread.

She and Kristen huddled together, away from the chattering, laughing kids. "Only nine showed up for the reunion," Kristen said softly.

"No sign of Marlin," April said, frowning.

"Did you notice? There's one kid missing from each team," Kristen said.

April shivered again. "I have the worst feeling about this," she told Kristen. "I really didn't want to come back here. Do you think something terrible is going to happen? Do you think we are in danger?"

Kristen shrugged. "What could happen?" she replied. "It's all a TV show—right?"

A few miles away, the sun beat down on the island. The palm trees swayed in a hot breeze.

Donald Marks stood near the top of the hill of blue rocks. He gazed at the cave opening, dark as night. Like a gaping black hole in the world, he thought.

Then he turned to Katherine, who stood on a rock ledge above him. Despite the heat, her blue cloak was wrapped tightly around her.

Her blond-brown hair fluttered in the breeze. Her

silvery eyes narrowed on him. "Well?" she sneered at him.

Marks wiped sweat from his bald head. "I'm keeping my part of the bargain, Katherine," he said, returning her stare. "I'm keeping my promise. I'm bringing your daughter back to the island."

Katherine smiled bitterly. "Now, at last, I will have my revenge."

TO BE CONTINUED . . .

Take a look at what's ahead in

THE NIGHTMARE ROOM
Thrillogy #3
No Survivors

April leaned close to Kristen. "Are we the only ones who aren't here to have a good time?" she whispered.

Kristen nodded. "No one else realizes the danger. . . ."

April turned as everyone started to cheer. Donald Marks came lumbering across the sand, followed by Mira and Blake, his two new assistants.

All three of them wore khaki shorts and white T-shirts with ACADEMY STAFF printed on the front in bold, black letters.

Marks was the director of The Academy. He was a huge man with a round, bald head and bushy black eyebrows over round, dark eyes.

He had a bulging stomach that bounced as he strode over the sand to the campfire. And a booming voice that came from deep in his belly.

He stepped into the circle of kids, wiping sweat off his broad forehead with a handkerchief. "Hot night," he said. "It's great to see you all. Great to be back on the island."

The video crew member with the blond ponytail moved in close to Marks. Marks waved him back. "No close-ups—please!" he said, laughing.

He turned back to the circle of kids. "I hope you will all just act natural. Ignore the cameras, okay? It won't be easy. They are everywhere. But just pretend these guys don't exist."

That will be hard for Pam, April thought. She has been following the video guys around since the moment we arrived.

"You're all going to be TV stars," Marks said, grinning at them. "We are going to hold our Life Games competitions again for the cameras. And once again, there is a big cash prize to the winner."

Everyone except April and Kristen cheered at that announcement. I don't care about winning more money, April thought. I just want to learn what is really going on here.

"Are you going to make new teams?" Clark asked, shouting over the crackling campfire. "Some kids are missing."

Marks mopped his forehead again. "We have some changes in the rules to make the games more exciting this time," he announced. "No teams. Everyone is on his own."

That brought another big cheer.

A grin spread over Marks's round face. "Watch out," he said. "Because of the TV cameras, we've added more excitement—and more danger."

"How is it more dangerous?" Kendra asked.

Marks stepped closer to the fire. The darting flames cast an orange glow over his face. His tiny, round eyes reflected the light.

He lowered his voice as if sharing a secret. "We have someone new on the island," he said. "We are not alone here anymore."

He grinned into the video camera. "We have a witch living on the island," Marks said. "You will recognize her by her blue cloak."

April felt a chill freeze her back.

Marks's grin grew wider. "If you see her—run!" he declared. "She isn't friendly. In fact, she is your enemy."

It grew very silent. Even the fire seemed to hush.

"Every day," Marks continued, speaking softly, "the witch is going to eliminate one contestant. Until there is only one of you left."

Some kids laughed. Others muttered to each other.

"Ooh, a real witch. I'm scared! I'm scared!" Anthony cried. He shook all over, pretending to be frightened.

"Maybe she'll turn you into a frog!" Kendra joked.

"She already did!" a boy named Phil shouted.

That made everyone laugh.

April turned to Kristen. "I don't believe it. Marks is making a joke of it," she whispered.

Kristen nodded. "He wants everyone to think the witch is part of the TV show. But *we* know she is real. And dangerous."

"We—we can't let him get away with this," April whispered. "We have to warn everyone. We have to let them know the danger is real."

Across the fire, Pam jumped to her feet. "Do I just have to watch?" she asked Marks. "I know I wasn't here the first time. But can I play in the games too?"

"Yes, you can," Marks replied. "Since some of the kids didn't make it—"

"Where are they?" April broke in. The words sounded more shrill than she had intended. "Where *are* Marlin, Dolores, and Jared? Do you know why they didn't come to the reunion?"

Marks's grin faded as he turned to April. "I invited them," he replied. "But I didn't hear back. I really don't know why they didn't want to come, April. I just don't know."

He's lying, April knew.

I can tell that he is lying. And why is he staring at me like that?

Is he trying to warn me to shut up? To stop asking about those missing kids?

Later, April and Kristen waited until all the lights were out in Marks's cabin. Then they ran quickly to the other cabins, waking kids up, dragging them outside.

April led them all down to the beach. Past the purple embers of the dying campfire. Around a bend out of sight of The Academy Village.

Moonlight poured down on the frothy waves as they splashed over the shore. A warm, salty breeze fluttered April's hair.

"April? What's the big idea?" Anthony asked. "I

was already asleep."

"Is this being taped?" Phil asked, looking around.

"Kristen and I want to talk to you," April began. "We think Marks is lying. About the missing kids."

"Oh, wow. Here we go again," Anthony groaned, rolling his eyes.

"Let her talk," Clark said.

"But she's crazy!" Anthony insisted.

"We're not crazy," Kristen broke in. "Something very strange has been happening to us."

"Back home," April said. "Things from the island followed us home.

"I had nightmares about the island every night," April told them. "They were so real. And I saw the woman in the blue cloak. She isn't pretend. In fact, she's dangerous."

"All kinds of disturbing things happened to me too," Kristen said. "How about the rest of you?"

"Yes. Did anyone else have frightening things happen to them?" April asked.

To her shock, *everyone* raised a hand.

"Oh, wow," April gasped. "We *all* were cursed!"

Silence again. Except for the whisper of the wind and the steady rush of waves against the rocky shore.

The kids still had their hands raised. And then, as they lowered them, they burst out laughing.

It took April a few seconds to realize they had all been joking.

"April, don't you ever give up?" Anthony demanded.

"Do you really believe in evil witches?" Kendra asked. "Like in fairy tales?"

April grabbed Anthony's arm. "You heard the woman singing. We *all* heard her. Remember?"

"Of course I remember," Anthony said, tugging free of her grasp. "It was part of the Bravery test. None of it was real, April. It was all a game."

"It wasn't a game!" April insisted.

Clark groaned. "Did you really wake us up and drag us down here for this?"

April balled her hands into tight fists. "Don't any of you realize that three kids are missing?" she cried. "We spoke to Marlin's mom. She said he never came home!"

"That's crazy," Kendra muttered.

Pam stepped up to April, her long blond hair fluttering in the wind. "I know what you're doing," she said. "You're trying to make yourself the center of attention."

"Huh?" April gasped. "Me? Why? Why would I do that?"

"To get the most camera time," Pam said. "You went on all those TV shows back home because you won the Life Games. And you really got to like being a big star—didn't you?"

"Whoa. Wait a minute—" April started.

"So now you want to be the star of this show too," Pam accused.

"I—I don't believe you!" April gasped.

"Lighten up, everyone," Clark said. "We're here

to have fun—right? We're here to party!"

"Yeah! Party! Party!" The kids started to chant.

Kristen pulled April aside. "Forget it," she whispered. "They're not going to believe us. They think it's all fun and games."

April stayed behind on the beach after the others finally returned to their cabins. The wind off the ocean carried a late-night chill. And the moon blinked in and out behind thin wisps of cloud.

Hugging herself to stay warm, April turned and gazed at the rock hills down the beach. The rocks glowed blue against the darkness.

So strange, April thought, hugging herself tighter. Even at night the rocks glow.

She remembered how cold they were to the touch. Even with the tropical sun pounding down on them, the rocks were always cold.

And somewhere at the top of those rocks lived a woman in a blue cloak.

A terrifying woman who sucked the breath out of her victims.

A woman whose evil magic had followed April home.

"I know you're there," April whispered. "The others may laugh. But I know the truth."

A sudden chill made April spin away. She started to jog back to her cabin. Her sneakers smacked the wet sand.

She turned from the beach, running through the

tall grass that led to the rows of cabins. She stopped when she saw the long object in the grass.

Was it moving?

Breathing hard, she bent to see it better.

At first, she thought it was a stick or a rolled-up palm tree leaf.

"Oh—!" April cried out when she saw that it was a long, pale snake.

Before she could step back, the snake raised its head from the grass.

April saw its eyes dart back and forth. She saw its tongue flicker.

And then it opened its jaw and hissed at her. "*No sssssurvivors*."